The Darcys

Scenes from Married Life

PHYLLIS FURLEY

Published 2004 by Egerton House Publishing
Egerton House, 3 Egerton Road, Bexhill on Sea,
East Sussex, TN39 3HH
THE DARCYS – SCENES FROM MARRIED LIFE
After Jane Austen's Pride and Prejudice
This edition first published 2004

ISBN NUMBER: 0-9546275-7-1

For David

Acknowledgements:

Many people have helped me in various ways during the writing of this book.

My first debt is to my friend, Caroline Champlin, who, before her tragically early death in 2000, provided years of friendly encouragement and constructive criticism.

My family, aided by my friend, Clifton Scott, made invaluable comments, in addition to struggling with my rudimentary computer skills and certain vagaries in my punctuation. On some occasions I may have eluded their vigilance.

Above all, I must record my thanks to Juliette Shapiro of Egerton House Publishing. She offered unstinting help, guidance, and the pleasures of reciprocal friendship.

In the interests of historical accuracy, Lord Saye and Sele kindly allowed me to describe the Darcys' visit to Broughton in a rare period of decay. The description stands in dramatic contrast to its present condition. On Open Days, I am a frequent visitor to that lovely castle and can attest to its excellent state of preservation.

Victor Gollanz Ltd. permitted me to use an illustration from: *Mrs Hurst Dancing – and other scenes from Regency Life 1812-1823*. Text by Gordon Mingay. Watercolours by Diana Sperling.

The Scenes are set at, or in the vicinity of-

LONGBOURN
PEMBERLEY
THE DARCYS' LONDON HOUSE
BROUGHTON CASTLE
LYME – a seaside resort
TOLLINGTON COURT – home of Colonel & Mrs Fitzwilliam
DUFTON HALL – home of Charles & Jane Bingley

Happy for all her maternal feelings was the day on which Mrs Bennet got rid of her two most deserving daughters. With what delighted pride she afterwards visited Mr Bingley and talked of Mrs Darcy may be guessed.

(PRIDE and PREJUDICE: by Jane Austen)

Scene One - Prelude

*T*he short season of courtship preceding the union of Elizabeth Bennet and Fitzwilliam Darcy had its difficulties and disappointments. Although he now maintained an unshakeable composure when confronted by the vulgarity of her mother and younger sisters, he had relied on time spent at Netherfield with Jane and Bingley to provide an agreeable alternative to Longbourn. A degree of patience was required before the benefits became apparent, due to the frequency with which Mrs Bennet chose to join the Netherfield party – inspired by curiosity about the absent Miss Bingley's domestic arrangements.

Fortunately, after a few days she suppressed this interest, being overtaken by nervous fears that she confided to her husband.

"I shan't have one moment's peace, Mr Bennet, until these marriages have taken place. It is all so strange, Mr Darcy suddenly making an offer to Lizzy after never having a word to say to her. Even *you* must admit she is not Jane's equal in beauty, and no-one could call her manners encouraging, particularly compared with the way Miss Bingley put herself out to be so attentive to Darcy. Remembering what I suffered during that terrible business of Jane being left in the lurch by Bingley, just when we felt assured of him, I am tormented with nightmares about Darcy regretting his odd choice and bolting to London, dragging Bingley with him again. Last time it lasted months on end,

13

without a word of explanation; but I try to reassure myself that Jane is finally secure of Bingley, so having the other couple mainly in their company might keep Darcy up to the mark."

"Mrs Bennet, while you may feel confident that in general our opinions coincide, as it happens we have never managed to agree about Lizzy's qualities; be assured Darcy knows what he is about, and the same is true of Bingley, now he has found the strength to defy his sisters."

His wife, unimpressed by her husband's views, followed her own plans, announcing to the two couples, "The four of you such good friends and choosing a double wedding! I suggest you enjoy yourselves by spending the days together at Netherfield before returning to Longbourn for dinner. You can chaperon each other, though I daresay Lizzie and Mr Darcy will be off on some of those long walks while Jane and Bingley are planning all their household arrangements. To my mind, there's nothing improper in that. I wish I could visit one more time to remind myself of all the offices and bedchambers and give Jane the benefit of my advice, but we must remember that Miss Bingley, even in her absence, is still mistress of the house. I am sure I would not like...."

This unusual delicacy, in Mrs Bennet, was prompted by the ever-present thought that, on Mr Bennet's death, she and her children could be immediately evicted from Longbourn in favour of Mr Collins, who had been snared by Charlotte Lucas (in an outrageously underhand manner) as soon as Lizzy refused him. Mrs Bennet had considered it quite understood that, to make some recompense for inheriting the entail in some devious way, his choice, after Lizzy, would naturally be the next available Bennet daughter,

Mary. For several minutes her conversation continued on these wearisomely familiar lines.

To the relief of her elder daughters, she finally returned to the welcome suggestion that their daytime hours should be passed at Netherfield with Bingley and Darcy. Knowing that the harsher winter of Derbyshire awaited her, Elizabeth was particularly anxious to enjoy the relatively mild November in Hertfordshire, and what could be more attractive for lovers than to be alone together examining the misunderstandings of the past and planning their future happiness? During these affectionate conversations they had no desire to touch upon difficulties that already existed or were likely to arise. As this was to be a union between two people raised in entirely dissimilar ways and whose natures were complementary rather than similar, it was an encouraging fact that, at present, there was but one misunderstanding causing genuine difficulties. Elizabeth felt it could be dispelled in a moment if Darcy would take the initial action. Why was he so unusually hesitant?

This uncharacteristic hesitancy also extended to a less immediate problem, one to which Elizabeth was happily oblivious: Darcy disliked her long-established habit of solitary rambles. With the lack of consistency to which all human nature is subject, he treasured a memory from those early days at Netherfield. Elizabeth Bennet had arrived, after walking three miles across fields, and enchanted him with the brightness of her eyes and complexion and caused him to excuse the muddy petticoat which later drew the scornful attention of Bingley's sisters. The recollection remained dear to him, even though he now decided that such activities were unsuitable for his wife. He assumed that changed circumstances would bring such things to a natural end, not realising that Elizabeth was ill prepared for the distinction he intended to make between a Miss Bennet and Mrs Darcy.

The happy arrangement of passing some of the daylight hours at Netherfield with Jane and Bingley lasted scarcely a week before Caroline Bingley announced her intention to return within a few days. Her hasty departure had been caused by the unwelcome intelligence of her brother's engagement to Jane, and was further extended by the even more painful news that Darcy had chosen Elizabeth Bennet in preference to herself.

"True affection brings her back to help her brother make everything ready before our marriage," Jane generously suggested. "Charles and I have enjoyed looking over the house on our own, but as you know, we are not going to settle here permanently; perhaps only for one more rental year. We are still not mentioning it to anyone else, but even before our engagement Charles' own inclination had been to move somewhat nearer to Pemberley."

"And now..." said Elizabeth, happy to leave the sentence unfinished while privately thinking: not only nearer Pemberley, but satisfactorily farther from Longbourn.

Jane had moved on to the subject of Bingley's family.

"Of course I can never again consider Caroline a *true* friend since learning of her determination to separate her brother from me, but she did write a generous letter of congratulation."

"Yes, that is the case, and she even succeeded in the more difficult task of achieving a very properly phrased letter to *me*. Nevertheless, she will be no more inclined to keep my company than I am to keep hers, and certainly *Mr Darcy* has ceased to be a welcome companion to her. Now he will be forced to develop an enthusiasm for seeing me at Longbourn, returning to Netherfield only to sleep."

As Jane would never enter into overt criticism of other members of their family, the sisters sat in silence while Elizabeth considered, and rejected, the advisability of consulting Jane about the strange barrier remaining between herself and Darcy.

During those leisurely country walks, Darcy's ardent gaze and tender words were never translated into any action beyond solicitously adjusting her wraps if they became disarranged. Elizabeth's belief that such reserve exceeded the decorum usually expected of an engaged couple was upheld by Jane's example. (When the four of them were together *she* allowed Bingley to put his arm round her waist, or confidently possess himself of her hands for kisses, those he obviously meant to bestow elsewhere as soon as they were alone.)

Although distinctly disappointed that her unspoken encouragement had no effect on her lover's undemonstrative behaviour, Elizabeth struggled not to allow it to mar their happiness.

Unfortunately this reasonable decision was not easily maintained, being opposed by painful recollections connected with Wickham – a man for whom Darcy justly felt an abhorrence even greater than her own. Many months ago there had been a disastrous period when Elizabeth had been beguiled by him; it would take time to forgive herself this foolishness, but she had decided that Darcy's first embrace would easily consign to oblivion one particularly uncomfortable memory. As no such balm had yet been offered, against her will her thoughts kept returning to that brief episode bringing all the attendant pain of once again confronting her own ill-judged preferences. Wickham had *then* appeared entirely delightful, Darcy entirely odious.

Considering the society available in Meryton, it was hardly surprising that a few (uninvited and clumsily bestowed) kisses had been the sum of Elizabeth's previous romantic experience. From age sixteen, when she graduated to the status of young lady, Miss Elizabeth Bennet had, more or less successfully, kept amorous men at a suitable distance, until, four years later she chose to offer no resistance to Mr Wickham when he held her in his arms for several minutes in a deserted antechamber. He had already charmed everyone with his pleasing manners and happy readiness in conversation, but it was to Elizabeth he devoted his attentions, bringing her at that moment dangerously close to falling in love with a man as penniless as she herself.

Undoubtedly an attraction existed on both sides, but too soon, he had turned his attention to a young woman suddenly endowed with ten thousand pounds. Not without initial pain, she reluctantly conceded that he needed a wife with some fortune. While judging him more kindly than she judged Charlotte Lucas for accepting Mr Collins for equally mercenary motives, she felt no inclination to watch Wickham courting Miss King.

To escape the situation she decided to visit the Collins' parsonage in Kent. A promise reluctantly given when Charlotte married, now presented itself as a blessed escape from Meryton society - even with the realisation that to the tedium of her host would be added the condescension of Lady Catherine de Bourgh, his esteemed patron. Elizabeth's enthusiasm for the plan was tested when Charlotte's hospitable reply was accompanied by insufferable advice from Mr Collins about the degree of deference to be shown to Lady Catherine. Particularly enraging was his recommendation of flattering references to the honour of being acquainted with her nephew, Mr Darcy.

While heartily disliking both men, for a moment Elizabeth had felt that the arrogance of one was almost preferable to the servility of the other, until recollecting the former's dishonourable behaviour to her friend Wickham. Notwithstanding the abruptness with which he transferred his attentions to Miss King, Elizabeth found herself disinterested enough to wish him well married, hoping that a settled future might compensate for any past injustice. Clearly, her deepest feelings had not been involved; she had escaped being in love, but he would remain in her memory a remarkably agreeable man with only minor faults of character.

In Kent, where she had the misfortune to encounter Mr Darcy once again, all her settled prejudices were challenged. The angry reasons she provided for rejecting his insultingly worded proposal of marriage, stung him into defending his actions over the many years of Wickham's connection with his family. Incontestable proof of her favourite's debauchery and mendacity was intensely painful, especially when she was forced to concede that the behaviour of the self-righteous Mr Darcy, whatever his faults of pride, had been both honourable and generous.

Humbled by the realisation that vanity, not discrimination, had formed her views of the two men, it was almost punishment enough to know she must see Wickham again. But a sudden stroke of fortune (welcomed by Elizabeth as fervently as it was mourned by the other young ladies of Meryton) almost immediately dispatched the Militia to the south coast. It was an additional relief that Miss King's guardians denied his suit and removed their ward to an undisclosed address.

Scarcely two months later came the dreadful news from Brighton that Wickham, decamping from his debts, had been accompanied by Elizabeth's sister, Lydia, a headstrong sixteen-year-old whose passions overwhelmed any shred of sense she might possess.

Elizabeth Bennet had scornfully refused Fitzwilliam Darcy's offer of marriage, but even so, for her sake and without her knowledge, he accepted all the mortifications involved in seeking out a man he justly despised, and by offering him further financial assistance - persuading him to marry Lydia. Such nobly unselfish actions exceeded any of the eulogies offered by Mr Collins, whose standard of excellence was solely concerned with birth and wealth.

Elizabeth's brief preference for Wickham might soon have been forgotten were it not for those memorable kisses. Looking back, she blamed herself for manners that encouraged such attentions, and conversely, she now felt provoked that her encouragement brought no change to Darcy's mode of courtship. His feelings she never doubted; they were apparent every moment in his eyes, his voice, the way he drew her arm through his and held her hand against his heart, or pressed it to his cheek. But a lover's kisses – such as she had received from Wickham - were still withheld. There were moments when her teasing spirit inclined her to take action herself, but imagining the scene brought a smile, for their difference in height made it likely she would reach no higher than his neckcloth.

Laughter was followed by renewed composure. Assured of his love, time would resolve this problem, as it would also solve the other puzzle of which name to use. Fitzwilliam seemed awkward, being unalterably associated with his cousin Colonel Fitzwilliam. Even when used as a family Christian name it still seemed as much a surname as Darcy – and Darcy came so naturally to her for private and public use.

Having rejected the unlikely possibility that her dear Darcy was a timid lover, Elizabeth was at a loss for any other solution. She had too little experience of the masculine world to fathom the complicated reactions of a man violently in love. In Darcy's sense of honour there was a particular nicety requiring him to disclose his amorous past before claiming the rights of an accepted lover. Yet he delayed, although it should be done as soon as possible, for Elizabeth's enticing manners became increasingly difficult to resist.

Usually a man of decisive action, the recollection of past misunderstandings between them made Darcy strangely diffident in the most important relationship of his life. There was an innocent charm about the early stages of their courtship that he feared would be lost when the extent of his past amours (of which he had no reason to feel ashamed) was revealed. Yet he longed to offer the closer embraces which she invited by every means other than speech.

Forced to be apart for a week while she, and Jane, visited London warehouses with Mrs Bennet and he, Darcy, supervised details of her welcome at Pemberley, they missed each other as intensely as if they had spent many months in the closest companionship. Returning soon after daybreak, Darcy's impatience made him an early visitor at Longbourn where he was lucky enough to find Elizabeth alone in the shrubbery while the rest of the household prepared for breakfast. They ran towards each other, his self-imposed restrictions were clearly forgotten, and after simultaneously embracing, laughing, and talking, gradually grew coherent.

"My own beloved Elizabeth! Propriety demanded that I tell you something of my past life before taking you in my arms, but I cannot regret a moment such as this."

Elizabeth, surprised, but reassured, by the knowledge that those discouraging formalities in his courtship were due to unfathomable rules of masculine behaviour, replied, "I feel only joy, with nothing of regret. Losing you for a week was as sad a deprivation as if we had been parted in our first few weeks of marriage. Until this separation I had not fully understood how closely bound together our lives already are. As for your gentlemanly sense of propriety, I am sorry you waited even these few weeks, but if there are words *you* feel should be spoken, this is the perfect time. Nothing you tell me can alter my feelings, and indeed I can hardly believe anything you say will seriously discompose me. I accept the inevitable fact that you have lived in a world unknown to me, while my *whole* life has always been what you see now."

With unusual impetuosity Darcy almost broke into her last words. "If only we could be married tomorrow! Waiting is intolerable. Although I admit to having business on your behalf at Pemberley last week, from this moment I wish all delays could be brought to a summary end, leaving us free to begin our real lives."

"I agree with all my heart. The past is nothing compared with the future. But if you still wish to talk about the years before we met...?"

Giving a strong affirmative, Darcy began, "Part of what follows may surprise you. A degree of reserve, already natural to me, was increased by boyhood experiences, and, as I grew towards manhood, helped to disguise my strongly amorous inclinations. At Oxford I made some estimable friends, but as it happened, was also introduced into the dissolute Carlton House set, which to my youthful inexperience seemed alluringly glamorous – the women in particular. When scarcely seventeen I was seduced by an acclaimed beauty twice my age, and for a few years thereafter was flattered to find myself a favourite among married women with complaisant husbands.

"I tell you this, Elizabeth, with no sense of shame; such behaviour did not involve subterfuge or deceit, but was an accepted rite of passage. My sense of chivalry has always been primarily concerned with young unmarried women. Above all I would never descend to the seduction of shop girls, or of female servants who (however provocative their manners) deserve the protection of their employers. Towards young women of my own class I was always circumspect by choice, hating the manoeuvres, transparent or disguised, resorted to in pursuit of an eligible husband. Alas, I must admit these encounters were frequent enough to reinforce my already inflated sense of superiority.

"There is little more to add, except that in my heart I was increasingly doubtful of finding what I most desired – a woman to whom I could offer my life-long devotion. The few handsome, intelligent, unaffected, women I met happened not to appeal to my strongest affections - hardly surprising considering how many diverse and incalculable elements are involved. What is inexcusable is my reluctance to admit that I loved you almost as soon as we met. Then came that fateful moment at Rosings when I belatedly declared my love and was deservedly and painfully rebuffed."

In theory well prepared for the different standards of behaviour expected of single men and women, Elizabeth experienced a brief twinge of amusement when comparing her anxiety about one ill-judged embrace with the scale of Darcy's experience. But that reassuring claim, made only minutes ago, that nothing would upset her, was incorrect; she felt dismayed. Her first impressions had condemned Darcy as unvaryingly cold and selfish, while later involvement disclosed his excellent principles and loving heart; neither of these conflicting views prepared her to hear of a profligate youth.

In an unspecified way she had expected a statement of discreet encounters, possibly arranged by a wise elder. His confession of ardent passions disassociated from affection shocked her. Reason almost immediately forced an admission that the relationships she had vaguely imagined would have been equally loveless, and therefore equally culpable – or equally acceptable according to the standards being applied. Vague but confusing visions of worldly women experienced in the arts of love so undermined her usual confidence that she chose not to refer to them, offering instead a half-smiling observation that Miss Bingley must be a prime example of an 'eligible young woman.'

"Your remark, a few days ago, that I had become sickened by assiduous attentions, partially accounts for my reactions to the social life of Meryton. Charles was delighted with his new role of country gentleman living on his own estate (albeit rented) and talked of settling there. But when we first arrived it seemed that, apart from his family, I would be the only guest and therefore essential to all his daily pursuits - Mr Hurst being no kind of companion. Unfortunately, that also made me the only object of interest to Miss Bingley. Fending off the attentions of my hostess while maintaining appropriate civility was a wearisome occupation."

As Elizabeth had frequently observed Caroline Bingley choosing to ignore the chilly brevity of his responses, she silently assented.

"This, a little, explains," he continued, "if it cannot excuse, the attitude I brought to the Meryton Assembly, expecting nothing agreeable while secretly longing for some worthwhile encounter. Seeing Charles enchanted by 'the beautiful Miss Bennet' only encouraged my critical attitude to all other representatives of local society, this view being repeated and embroidered by the ladies in my party. On that disastrous first evening I even managed to dismiss the lively charms...."

Darcy paused briefly until reassured by Elizabeth's fond look.

"Well, I was properly punished for my unforgivably audible comment, and while ever more fascinated by you, was unwillingly thrown back on the studied compliments and artificial conversation of my hostess. I was a lamb being prepared for the slaughter."

"Not a convincing analogy," protested Elizabeth, "Caroline Bingley was an unsuccessful huntress shooting her arrows ever wider of the mark."

"While I was a man increasingly bewitched against his will."

"A condition well disguised from me."

"Not from *her*, however; it was a Comedy of Errors now happily resolved."

On this cheerful note the conversation ended. Elizabeth rejoiced that she had concealed the unease she felt about the earlier experiences he described, and Darcy was equally pleased with what appeared to be her untroubled reaction to them. Fully confident of loving and being loved, he renewed his passionate declaration of fidelity.

Returning to the house, the inevitably banal conversation at breakfast made them long for escape. Darcy felt he was truly paying off arrears of civility by enduring Mrs Bennet's voluble details of warehouses already patronized and those still awaiting a visit.

"My dear Mr Darcy, it is all very well for you romantic lovers, but not nearly enough time has been left for these essentials. It is hard for me with the needs of two daughters to attend to, and heaven knows this visit to London was no pleasure in my state of nerves, but what with the date being set so early, the girls inevitably depended on their mother, although my sister Gardiner volunteered her help."

Jane and Elizabeth smiled politely, whatever their private opinions as to the veracity of these statements, but Kitty, indifferent to niceties of behaviour, shrugged her shoulders and rolled her eyes upward, earning a sharp reproof. If she could not achieve the ladylike deportment of her elder sisters she was most unlikely to enjoy a future in any way resembling theirs.

An improved understanding rather than improved deportment was required, thought Mr Bennet, uneasily conscious of his own negligence. Already fatigued by his wife's infelicities, he made no effort to deflect the conversation into more rational channels, but secured his own escape by withdrawing to his study.

To counteract months of open antagonism to Darcy, Mrs Bennet continued her efforts to ingratiate herself with the dazzling marital prize her least favourite daughter had so surprisingly won. If dimly aware that a conversation centred on shopping and her state of health would not appeal to most men (Mr Bennet having taught her this much) she nevertheless found it hard to abandon subjects so dear to her heart. Furthermore she was mistakenly encouraged by the concentrated gaze Darcy fixed upon her – which merely served to mask his total lack of attention. As Elizabeth was also absorbed in her own thoughts it was left to Jane to draw her mother's attention away from Darcy with an urgent query about one of the lengths of dress muslin.

Scene Two

In a double ceremony, Mr Bennet gave in marriage his daughter, 'Jane Frances, spinster of this parish, to Charles Hughes Bingley, Esquire, of Netherfield Park in this parish, and his daughter, Elizabeth Susan, spinster of this parish, to Fitzwilliam Thomas Augustus Darcy, Esquire, of Pemberley in the county of Derbyshire.'

As Lady Catherine de Bourgh was not among the small number of invited guests there was only Caroline Bingley to disapprove. In the unhappy position of deploring both marriages, she was forced to show a smiling face to Georgiana Darcy who looked forward, with intense pleasure, to joining her brother and new sister at Pemberley within the next few weeks. Everyone present agreed that, as to fortune, the two elder Bennet girls had done amazingly well, but those who really cared for them rejoiced in their prospects of true conjugal felicity.

Yet in the first weeks after their marriage, Elizabeth Darcy's confidence in her husband was not matched by equal self-assurance. She was uncertain of her own emotions which no longer seemed under her control; Darcy's love could not be doubted, but the contrast between his experience and her inexperience threatened her independent spirit.

Admiration and gratitude had transformed her feelings from dislike to love, but due to a recently acquired distaste for outward attractions, his handsome, manly appearance had been only a secondary consideration. To her surprised delight, that moderate assessment was swept away by the pleasures of married love, but confidence in her new life eluded her during days in which she had little to do. Freezing fog had caused Pemberley's steward to dislocate his shoulder by slipping on an icy path, resulting in Darcy spending more time in the Estate Office than he had planned; in fact few extra hours were involved, but combined with the hostile weather, Elizabeth felt the deprivation. As she had an exquisite pianoforte to use and an extensive library with which to become acquainted, she was annoyed to feel restless and unsettled when left to her own society. It was a surprise to find the early days of her marriage resembling the early days of her engagement, in that she *knew* that she was happy rather than *felt* herself to be so.

The domestic offices were visited under the housekeeper's jurisdiction, but she chose to wait until her husband could show her the extent of Pemberley beyond the rooms in daily use. Darcy was secretly gratified by Elizabeth's questions about the growth of the house through centuries, this being a particular interest of his own not yet acknowledged to her. However, that was nothing to the feelings he experienced when leading her through a range of attics that had provided a very young Fitzwilliam Darcy with an escape from the adult world and its incomprehensible problems.

On impulse he chose this moment to describe the tragic losses endured by his parents; of necessity Elizabeth must be told, although it was a disturbing story to inflict upon a newly married young woman. Taking her hand, he explained that, following his birth and continuing into the years after Georgiana's, there had been a number of babies stillborn or surviving only a few weeks or months. Aged six and eight he had attended two funerals, but otherwise knew little more than the memorials she would see in the family chapel on Sunday. He was a dearly cherished only child, but, inevitably, parental love was anxious rather than joyful. Behind his carefully controlled words Elizabeth heard the voice of that small boy retreating alone to his attic hiding-place, and her wordless response was so tender, so immediate, that Darcy comforted her with the reminder that these sad events were many years in the past.

Almost in silence they looked into nooks and crannies where Elizabeth was disappointed in her hope of finding some well-used toys or books, apparently those worth retaining were all carefully packed away – how typical of the careful management at Pemberley. Then they turned their gaze to narrow windows providing partial views of angled turrets and balustrades, with Darcy helping his wife identify the glimpses of parkland beyond. Feeling calmer as they stepped through another door, Elizabeth pressed closer to her husband, asking for more recollections of his childhood, but he was briefly distracted from their embrace by the entry of two servants from a different direction. Although this was a situation he particularly disliked, he continued to hold his wife closely while reminding himself to be more controlled in future.

Used to the formal manners of his parents, Darcy assumed the new master and mistress of Pemberley, like their predecessors, would never make a public display of happiness; a reasonable assumption had he not taken such a narrow view of 'display.' Until this moment, Elizabeth had regretted a marked change between the spontaneity and unreserved nature of their hours alone together, and the daily routines of life during which Darcy offered her no more than the courteous attentions due to any woman. She even reflected (with some exaggeration) that Caroline Bingley would have received the same treatment!

A degree of reserve was seemly with servants in attendance, but she judged her husband made too great a concession to the solemn atmosphere already existing at Pemberley. Not only was it uncomfortable to find footmen posted like sentries in the saloon, the anteroom, the dining room, but Darcy's formal manners were also carried to excess. Yet she hesitated to initiate changes so soon, particularly with her own spirits tiresomely unsettled.

Following that momentary embrace, she now hoped a reasonable display of affection could be shown in the presence of servants – joined to the further hope that in the near future there might be fewer of them in silent attendance. Feeling the moment to be appropriate she almost voiced her thoughts, then rejected the idea. They were only a few days married; no husband – certainly not one of Darcy's character – would welcome anything approaching criticism at this early stage. For the present the wisest, happiest, action was to understand the past before she tried to change anything.

Elizabeth's husband was gratified by her strong interest in Pemberley's past, though had he been able to deduce *all* her thoughts they might have won less approval. It is rare for any two people, however much in love, to completely understand each other, and though Darcy vaguely foresaw that Elizabeth might want to make changes, he imagined nothing more than minor alterations in furnishings or food.

In these boyhood recollections one name, George Wickham, was not mentioned, but Elizabeth realised that *he* had been the companion most frequently available, remaining a favourite of the elder Mr Darcy long after the son understood the specious nature of that youthful charm. While she had enjoyed all the benefits of an elder sister incapable of deceit, her husband had been obliged to enjoy the company of a boy who was a natural deceiver and manipulator. This must have driven young Darcy into habits of reserve, even with the father who was otherwise ideally formed to be his guide and confidant.

With what easy assurance, only a year ago, had Elizabeth laughingly claimed to be a student of human nature. Her husband was as complex an example as she was likely to encounter, his strong feelings being marked by his father's sympathetic benevolence, combined with a need to dominate and judge inherited from his mother's family, the Fitzwilliams. Discarding her earlier, frivolous approach, Elizabeth hoped to achieve greater understanding and thereby possibly exert a beneficial influence over a nature she now considered almost entirely admirable.

It was likely that just as many inconsistencies existed in her own character, but while reluctant to undervalue herself, Elizabeth felt naively transparent when compared with her husband. Even so, the radical changes in her life were bringing unexpected difficulties. Good sense and excellent intentions had prepared her for numerous adjustments before the new Mr and Mrs Darcy could become the happiest of married couples, but the shock of removal from everything made familiar over two decades of life came as a surprise.

Full of joyful expectations of life at Pemberley, it seemed easy to bid farewell to her old home, especially as Jane was leaving at the same time, but she had mistakenly underestimated Longbourn's claims. Amid the pains and exasperations of a regrettably disharmonious household, life had, on balance, been good. In addition to Jane's incomparable company, there had been books, music, the countryside, and particular corners of the house and grounds that were as dear to her as Darcy's attics were to him. With the support of a beloved father and elder sister she had been happy enough, until her critical faculties forced her to admit she could neither love nor respect her mother and that her father was a grossly irresponsible parent to his younger daughters.

When entering upon '...all the comfort and elegance of their family party at Pemberley...' she believed herself ready to adapt to the modes of life already established there. All this was rationally understood, but just as she had underestimated the claims of Longbourn, she was no better prepared for the power exerted by her new home. While approving of almost everything, and having absolutely no inclination to interfere with the housekeeper, she was uneasy with her daytime role as a mere appendage.

For a week, exceptionally stormy weather (bringing everything but snow) permitted only an occasional stroll from the terraces to the shrubbery or the walled gardens. Whenever the wind veered to a more friendly quarter, broader walks on well-maintained drives were available, but, as she confessed to Darcy, mixed with her genuine appreciation of their variety, was the lure of that wilder countryside only briefly explored during her first visit to Derbyshire. She had no serious wish to venture into those high moors at such a season, but even mentioning the idea did no service to her general hopes of roaming freely.

"My dear, in these conditions it would not be feasible even if I came with you. Neither the steward nor I would consider sending experienced estate workers up those narrow tracks unless essential maintenance required it. You do not understand how rapidly the climate changes. No, the level paths must be enough for now – and I suggest in general. I hope you will soon choose riding as the rational mode of going further afield; we can ride together as often as not."

Of course Elizabeth agreed.

"That will be the happiest choice of all, but in clement weather, when you are not available, I would be sorry to lose the right to walk out with no greater preparation than changing my shoes and announcing where I'm going. For the moment there is no doubt that either fog or frost make the steep paths dangerous, but those moorland crags - so familiar to you – entice me. You forget I had no more than a glimpse of them before last summer's excursion with the Gardiners was interrupted."

A general sense of unease, manifested by her husband's continuing silence, caused a change of tone.

"During the current spell of foul weather, how grateful I am that the tithe barn provides an indoor riding ring. Having lessons on my own beautiful mare has nothing in common with ambling around Longbourn on an elderly hack. I never could find pleasure in that, but now I concede that riding might almost equal the pleasures of walking, particularly when I become a suitable companion for you."

He warmly supported this thought, but did not add his additional reason: even if he were busy elsewhere there would always be a groom in attendance, in his view both safer and more seemly at any time of year. They said no more about Elizabeth's pleasure in solitary walks, Darcy being as reluctant to assert his power of prohibition as his wife was to resign a freedom she had always enjoyed and never abused. Each hoped for that unlikely result, a compromise satisfying two radically opposed ideas, but for the moment their mutual harmony was of paramount importance.

Georgiana would soon be joining them and Elizabeth already knew she was little interested in vigorous exercise, preferring a quiet drive in a carriage rather than riding or walking on unpaved tracks. Even allowing for her new sister's more sedentary inclinations, husband and wife agreed her companionship would be a great advantage, men and women inevitably having different occupations during some part of each day.

In these early days of their marriage, Elizabeth was sometimes taken to visit elderly or needy dependents. She felt very much an outsider in the Pemberley community when she heard an old couple absent-mindedly address her husband as 'Mr Fitzwilliam' (a name she had not yet brought herself to use) but she was, in fact, warmly welcomed. Darcy, knowing that that his wife's friendly manner set everyone at ease, hoped his sister might learn from her example. The Christmas visits all three of them would soon be making would provide a natural opening for the two young women to continue these activities in the future.

From the moment Georgiana arrived the sisters always spent part of each day together. Very often music engaged them, with Georgiana setting a good example by practicing seriously despite remaining fearful of performing for an audience.

Elizabeth's contribution to this new relationship encompassed much more. Painfully diffident, the younger girl had escaped from companions to the solitary pleasures of reading, but nowadays she delighted in sharing this pleasure by recommending particular favourites to her new sister. While appreciating

Georgiana's warm affections and good understanding, Elizabeth regretted that these qualities were combined with a lack of humour so complete she either failed to identify a joke, or looked anxious as if laughter might be subversive.

Georgiana was the true inheritor of Pemberley's sobriety. Her brother was not given to easy laughter, but during their engagement Elizabeth had learned to recognise, and rejoice in, a slight change of expression or a vestigial smile even if he chose not to respond actively. Georgiana was dutifully studious, Darcy, naturally clever and quick despite his stately manners.

Their family Christmas was a quiet joy to them all. The services in Pemberley's Church, followed by the gifts and feasts for servants and young children and, more importantly, the taking of comforts and delicacies to the elderly and sick, reminded them how exceptionally blessed were their own lives.

If at Pemberley happiness wore a serious face, in a short time this would be changed by the arrival not only of the Gardiners and the Bingleys (including Caroline) but all the Bennet family with the exception of Lydia and the infamous Wickham. When nearly all the preparations were made, they received the unwelcome news that Mr Gardiner's business would keep his family in London. Elizabeth was ashamed that her sharp regret was matched by equally strong feelings of relief when she heard that Lydia had persuaded her mother to return with them to Newcastle.

"Georgiana", said her brother at breakfast one morning, "You and Elizabeth performed that duet so flawlessly last night that I hope you have lost all fear of offering it to a wider audience."

They had been rehearsing with exactly this occasion in mind, with Elizabeth singing the descant while Georgiana had the piano to accompany her voice; even so, doubt was expressed.

"There are so many people who are almost strangers to me."

"But you will have Miss Bingley who is such an admirer of your music."

"I always feel unequal to her expectations. And the new Mrs Bingley, so esteemed by everyone, and... " Georgiana thought of Mr Bennet, whose manners were so unlike those of other gentlemen, but having murmured his name, embarrassment kept her silent.

Her brother continued, "Let me reassure you about Mrs Bingley; she is admired not only for beauty and dignity, but for unaffected good nature; she and Bingley are alike in that."

Elizabeth was gratified by her husband's praise of her beloved sister, but offered her own laughing comment.

"Jane is never censorious, and where music is concerned remains charmingly uncritical as she plays and sings very rarely. My sister Mary practises diligently, but talent is lacking so you will certainly outshine her. If it is my father of whom you are nervous, I assure you his quizzical comments are reserved for his family."

As she finished speaking she doubted her own words, wondering if the unfamiliar role of guest would increase his whimsical manner. He might well feel lost when deprived of the privacy of his own library.

Then there was the different problem of her younger sisters. In addition to stumbling through music that was too challenging, would Mary be inspired to a parade of learning by quoting ill-digested information? At least she could rely on Kitty to be mainly silent, in awe of Darcy and Pemberley and wishing she had been allowed to join Lydia in Newcastle among all the young officers. But there was a real danger that Caroline Bingley would coax her into gushing about the militia.

When Georgiana left the room Elizabeth offered Darcy her view of Miss Bingley, which he tried to soften.

"Perhaps you do her an injustice. Despite my earlier, unchivalrous, criticisms she no longer has any devious plans. I wonder, however, if expensive seminaries for young ladies do not replace simple ignorance with an insincerity and artificiality, which is infinitely worse. As joint guardians, my cousin and I agreed Georgiana had been long enough at school by the time she was fifteen. But I must also concede that another year with companions of her own age, foolish or not, might have made her more at ease in general society."

"Perhaps the admirable qualities shared by you and Jane are due to a rather random education leaving you free to educate each other? Your high standards and self-reliance must have developed from years of discussion between two young people blessed with natural goodness as well as intelligence."

Elizabeth insisted that all credit was due to Jane, which Darcy disputed before continuing.

"You have seen Miss Bingley at her worst. Obviously her manners to you will be amended. Her conversation should be much improved now she is no longer planning and contriving on behalf of her brother and herself - which I admit accounts for some of her great partiality for Georgiana, but not, I hope, all."

As his wife felt this merely served to illustrate Miss Bingley's hypocrisy, no further comment was made before Darcy went out to the stables, leaving Elizabeth to join Mrs Reynolds in an inspection of the accommodation prepared for the visitors, especially that of Caroline Bingley whose arrival was imminent.

All the other guests were expected the day after next, but she bore in mind that her father would disappoint settled expectations whenever possible. Jane and her husband were to use the large apartments soon be refurnished for Darcy and herself. At the present time it was a pleasure to share her husband's bachelor rooms, but his parents' apartments included a private sitting room into which servants would only come when summoned. She longed for the greater daytime privacy which would be achieved by this move, and little by little hoped to moderate in other ways the excessive formality observed by the elder Darcys.

Elizabeth looked forward to time alone with Jane before the other members of their family arrived, in part to discuss the problems caused by a domestic life totally unlike anything previously experienced. But she had to remind herself that perhaps no difficulties existed at Netherfield which was a recently rented home, less formally organised, and already familiar. As for Jane missing some aspects of her old life, she was more likely to find the proximity of Longbourn too close for married comfort.

More particularly Elizabeth wondered whether or not the Bingleys would welcome the likelihood of a first child within a year. She and Darcy wished to wait some months more before starting their family. All this depended on a strong element of luck as well as Darcy's knowledge, but it was not essential to their happiness; they could quickly become reconciled to early conception.

Elizabeth already rejoiced that the Bingleys were increasingly interested in purchasing their own estate in the near future. It would be altogether more comfortable for Jane if the move to a permanent home were to be made well before she faced childbirth. Half guiltily, Elizabeth corrected herself for planning not only Jane's home, but the appropriate date for her first child. It seemed Darcy was not the only person inclined to manage Charles Bingley's life.

The arrival of Bingley's sister interrupted these thoughts. Some initial embarrassment must be felt on all sides when the newly married couple received their first visit from Miss Bingley, though of the three people concerned Darcy suffered least, being the only one to know with absolute certainty that in no circumstances would he have proposed to Caroline Bingley.

The unfortunate woman had to endure being welcomed by the rival she had always detested – feelings well justified by the fact Elizabeth Bennet now filled the coveted position of Mistress of Pemberley. The visitor must even concede her place as the particular friend of Georgiana Darcy who had become wonderfully devoted to her new sister. Despite these powerful disadvantages, on mature consideration Caroline Bingley was still anxious to remain on good terms with her brother's intimate friend, Darcy of Pemberley, and consequently had prepared herself to say all that was obliging and insincere. Unlike Elizabeth, she at least enjoyed the advantage of being no stranger to duplicity.

"My dear Mrs Darcy, visits to beautiful Pemberley have always given great pleasure, but they will now be enhanced by your presence and the happy circumstances that you and I are connected through your dear sister's marriage to my brother."

Fortunately for Elizabeth, her guest avoided the ultimate insincerity of suggesting they were therefore nearly sisters. This was a battle in which Caroline Bingley had been roundly defeated. With her next words, Elizabeth struggled to show the magnanimity of a victor without being false to every natural feeling. It was not easy.

"I am delighted to see you, and particularly glad to welcome you at a time when Georgiana is also here to enjoy the pleasure of your company."

Knowing her listener's contempt for all the Bennet connections, including the Gardiners, she could not resist adding, "My father and younger sisters will arrive soon, which, with the addition of Jane and your brother, will complete our party. Sadly you are to be deprived of the company of my Aunt and Uncle Gardiner; business detains him in London."

When Georgiana had greeted her friend, the two Darcy ladies escorted their visitor to her apartments, which she delighted in recognizing as her usual rooms. Unlike the interlopers who would soon be arriving, she could at least boast a well-established knowledge of Pemberley. This puny victory was cheerfully conceded by Elizabeth, who willingly offered her other opportunities to make similar points.

Daylight had long vanished and dinner was over, when a man on horseback, hastily sent from the lodge, brought news that Mr Bennet's coach had entered the park and would soon be at the house. The business which detained him had been quickly dispatched, so seeing no reason to delay, Mr Bennet demanded rapid activity from his daughters as well as himself. By travelling hard they managed with only one overnight stop, and while their father was in fine spirits the two girls were fatigued and dishevelled after the long journey in bad weather.

Elizabeth was happy to usher them into the comforts of warm bedrooms and assure them of something to eat as soon as they were ready. Mr Bennet, who found one of his younger daughters vapid and the other pretentious, was delighted to be in Elizabeth's company again, and approved of Darcy's suggestion that he and his favourite child sit together in the library until his fellow travellers were ready to dine.

"So Lizzy you missed the festivities at Netherfield. Jane and Bingley were, of course, complaisant hosts, Lydia and her husband as confident and impudent as ever, and the two other girls inevitably foolish. Your mother was continually misunderstanding Miss Bingley's remarks, recognising the ill will but seizing on irrelevant details.

"Perhaps it is fortunate the Gardiners were unable to come; their intelligent conversation would have mixed ill with the stream of nonsense flowing over the Bingleys' uncomplaining heads. And, for the first time in your life, you may have some claim to be your mother's favourite child, at least in your absence. Mrs Bennet is very ready to visit the Bingleys, but possibly prefers talking about Mr and Mrs Darcy to actually visiting Pemberley."

Elizabeth felt a twinge of guilt.

"But my mother's decision to return to Newcastle with the Wickhams was very proper. Lydia is so heedless and rash that her mother's presence must increase her respectability among new acquaintance."

There was a lack of conviction in Elizabeth's voice as she offered this opinion; with some pain she compared Georgiana's upbringing with Lydia's, entirely to the disadvantage of the latter, until she recalled that her carefully nurtured sister-in-law had been equally ready to elope with Wickham. Mr Bennet, deducing the first part of her thoughts, watched her a minute in silence.

"You warned me Lydia was becoming fixed in ignorance and vanity, but Wickham's continuing determination to please every woman he meets may make her less vain, and I must do her the credit to say she is good-natured, even affectionate in her careless way, and never retreats into nervous attacks."

Depressed by her father's analysis of Lydia's character, even when absolving her of one of his wife's most irritating faults, Elizabeth was additionally pained by the dismissive tones in which he habitually spoke of his family. Jane's months of suffering under Bingley's neglect had only produced the comment that, next to being married a girl liked to be crossed in love a little. But then she remembered the real pleasure he later showed in Jane's happiness, and his anxious concern for her, Elizabeth, when he urged her not to marry Darcy unless she could truly love and respect him.

Strong winds and sleet kept them all within doors most of the following day, but father and daughter seized a calm period to walk on the gravel paths before Darcy and Mr Bennet rode further afield to look at new ditches and drainage. Mary announced her wish to go to the music room, but Elizabeth, knowing Georgiana was already there with the sycophantic Miss Bingley, settled her in the library before attending to Kitty, who had unsuccessfully struggled with her own hair rather than summon an unfamiliar maid. When Elizabeth volunteered her help, the sisters talked so comfortably that Kitty, whose character and tastes were easily swayed, began to feel that the society of Pemberley and Netherfield might have advantages despite the lack of officers.

Later that afternoon Kitty's self-assurance was high enough for her to start a conversation with Georgiana and Miss Bingley; the latter merely stared and inclined her head slightly, but Georgiana replied - almost audibly. As this was the most satisfactory communication the young ladies achieved, it was a pity

Elizabeth was too preoccupied to notice. She was distracted by fears that the heavy rain would delay the Bingleys, but they arrived, despite wheels deep in mud, within an hour of the expected time.

The sisters sat together in Jane's dressing room; both of them so obviously well and happy there was no need for enquiry. Instead, Elizabeth was immediately teased for resisting the cap suitable to her married status. Jane's womanly frame and classical features suited the headdress, but Elizabeth was in no hurry to adopt it.

"What are Darcy's thoughts?" Jane wondered. "I imagine him to be a supporter of tradition."

"In general you may be correct, but in this particular he is unconcerned – possibly because caps are somehow connected in his mind with housekeeping duties, but more straightforwardly are not to his taste, any more than large and elaborate hair ornaments. He argues," continued Elizabeth demurely, "that beautiful hair is more attractive than any head covering indoors."

"*Your* beautiful hair in particular. All these years I have endured rollers and rags while you had only to use a brush on your thick curls!"

The sisters smiled affectionately at each other remembering their shared girlhood, before Elizabeth was prompted to ask more about Christmas at Netherfield.

"You and Darcy were sadly missed, although I was happy to entertain my family. But I am not sure that our mother enjoyed being a guest instead of the hostess as much as she expected. She felt the lack of her sister Philips and the local people she always entertains at Longbourn, for despite all the preparatory work, she likes having those old friends around her."

A few carefully bland comments were added, before Jane continued.

"Our general ideas about removing from Netherfield are more specific now, for Bingley means to discuss with Darcy what properties he may know of within a reasonable distance from Pemberley. We will keep it just between the four of us until a place is found."

If not unexpected, the news was so delightful that Elizabeth's high spirits caused her to say, "To make *everything* comfortable perhaps you could find an acceptable husband for Caroline at a suitable geographical distance – an Irish Baronet who lives on his estates, or an outrageously rich West Indian planter, similarly situated?"

Even Jane's tender conscience allowed her to laugh as she modified Elizabeth's suggestion.

"About two hundred miles would be enough, for I do believe Charles to be as genuinely attached to her, as Caroline, very naturally, is to him. Once her ambitions are satisfied she will be a more comfortable companion for us all."

The hope of Jane living within easy reach made Elizabeth equal to all the strains of the evening. In fact, some open antagonism from Miss Bingley would have been preferable to unconvincing civilities surrounding the occasional barbed dart. When invited to offer some music, she enthused, "Dear Georgiana's piano! How well I remember the joy with which she received her brother's exquisite gift."

This remark caused surprise rather than pleasure to her young friend, who with Darcy's heartfelt approval, no longer thought of the instrument as her particular possession. After giving a polished performance Caroline not only suggested Mary Bennet take her place but repeatedly asked her to continue, much to Mary's gratification and the dismay of everyone else. Georgiana, assuming that nervousness produced these vocal discords, was amazed by the girl's courage.

At last, Mary was coaxed away and Elizabeth and Georgiana sang the duets they had been rehearsing. Caroline Bingley's evening was not to be one of unalloyed triumph. When she offered congratulations on their performance of Handel's *'Where'er You Walk,'* Georgiana confided, "I love the words because they make me think of Elizabeth."

Her listener looked uncomprehending, so Georgiana took her brother's arm to gain his attention,

"I am explaining this ill, but although the season is not appropriate, now Elizabeth is at Pemberley, *'All things flourish where'er you turn your eyes.'* We both agree about this, do we not, brother?"

Darcy could almost have felt a touch of pity for Miss Bingley, but his feelings were fully absorbed elsewhere. After smiling affectionately at his sister, he turned to his wife and with a rare gesture of gallantry raised her hand to his lips, then, apparently solicitous for his guests, decided that as the Bingleys had endured an uncomfortable journey through mud and rain they must be anxious to retire.

Possibly to the surprise of some other members of the party, he ordered candles for everyone, and all the guests were escorted to their rooms.

∘❧❧

Scene Three

∘❧❧

*T*he tensions caused by some of the guests throughout the next two weeks were greatly softened by Darcy and Elizabeth's pleasure in the company of the Bingleys. Darcy's realization that Jane was the perfect partner for Charles Bingley, entirely discredited his, Darcy's, earlier interference, yet the style of friendship between the two men had always encouraged the latter to be somewhat high-handed. In the eyes of the world Bingley gained most from the relationship, there being no disputing Darcy's greater social consequence, keener intellect, and stronger character. As usual, the truth was more complex; notwithstanding routine complaints about Bingley's lack of proper discrimination, Darcy envied the genial spirits which enabled his friend to enjoy almost any activity that choice or chance brought his way. The renewal of this masculine companionship continued to be a pleasure, although Elizabeth's buoyant nature, at the moment slightly subdued by new experiences, now softened his more sombre one.

Attending to the needs of the visitors inevitably turned Elizabeth's thoughts towards her wider role at Pemberley. She decided to discuss this with Mrs Reynolds, who had twenty years experience as housekeeper. In the lifetime of Darcy's parents she had grown used to having the family nearly always in residence, but after their deaths, had managed with equal efficiency during the frequent absences of the young master in his bachelor years.

Initially, Mrs Reynolds had felt anxious about adjusting to the wishes of the new Mrs Darcy, but Elizabeth claimed no greater involvement than approving the daily menus and inspecting the arrangements made for the comfort of guests. This morning they visited the rooms prepared for local people invited to a dinner in honour of the Bennets and the Bingleys. Despite the potential advantage of a full moon, most families would be staying overnight. These included a gentleman farmer who was Lambton's magistrate, another squire of ancient lineage accompanied by his many children, and three clerical families, also with grown-up children.

It was as well Mrs Bennet was absent. She would not have objected to them being described as worthy country neighbours rather than intimate friends, if only the word 'prosperous' had been included, but no young man in the party could be considered a possible husband for Mary or Kitty. Only one person was already known to Elizabeth – Mr Warriner, Pemberley's curate, who would go home after dinner to his small parsonage just beyond the park gates. This singular character, the son of an old friend of Darcy's father, devoted more time to the study of wild flowers than to clerical duties, and showed a child-like gentleness of manner. As his parishioners' material needs were already attended to, he had only to concern himself with their spiritual welfare, and in this area the Darcys themselves showed no inclination to consult him, while the Pemberley dependents seemed content with his generalised - if ineffectual - benevolence. He took pains to encourage the belief that his housekeeper managed his life for him.

The details of the house party being settled, Elizabeth asked Mrs Reynolds about Lady Anne Darcy's involvement in the larger world of Pemberley: estate workers, tenants, whole villages employed almost entirely by the Darcys.

"Well madam, my late mistress was rather an invalid, and although she and my late master mainly resided here, they lived very quietly. She was a great lady, always recognised as such, but very reserved you know, not having much to do with her inferiors, though with a sharp eye for any dishonesty or unsatisfactory service. Mr Darcy kept her well informed, but, while holding her in the greatest esteem, was inclined to be more tolerant of small failings. He took care to assure himself of the welfare of everyone he employed, and assisted other people too, where there was pressing need; the new master takes after his father in that. The family has always been compassionate, but not what you could call interfering - if you understand me."

Elizabeth was relieved to know that Lady Anne had not been an officious busybody like her sister Lady Catherine, even if equal in pride. While musing, she missed some of Mrs Reynolds' words, but was not encouraged by what she did hear.

". . . Sunday Schools. . . Mistress of Pemberley the patron; prizes for attendance and Catechism. . . Second generation of women doing fine needlework for ladies of Pemberley. . . much appreciated that you are giving them time to sew all your personal linen. . . a visit from you... training girls for service in respectable houses."

Elizabeth, poorly prepared in these areas, thanked Mrs Reynolds and promised further discussion. The Bennets had done very little charitable work, but as Mrs Darcy she must learn to be actively useful; perhaps she and Georgiana could work together? Her husband had tentatively suggested some shared commitments but apparently visualised Elizabeth in control. At first this seemed unsuitable; however extreme Georgiana's shyness, *she* knew these people and their connection with the family. Further reflection made his judgement appear correct rather than flattering.

Going in search of Jane to share her thoughts, she found her sister rearranging her cap, thus persuading Elizabeth to try on several of them as a suitable prelude to talking about new duties. She discarded them all with a laugh.

"*You* wear them and remain quite unchanged, but I am not yet convinced they are for me."

"Yet I think marriage has changed you Lizzie, although I can scarcely define it, and perhaps you would say the same about me."

"You are blooming with the happiness you have always deserved, but otherwise your manner is unaltered. If I have changed, undeserved happiness has brought it about, so why should it not be all to the good?"

"Because I, for one, would not want you to change. Although we are not always in full agreement about people, I miss your lively comments. Only one little joke about Miss Bingley so far."

"I lack material. I'm beginning to sigh for Mr Collins and Lady Catherine; it appears that happiness is a serious business."

"Oh, Lizzy, now I hope you *are* joking. However, you are right to the extent that Darcy's manner is naturally grave, and his presence strongly felt. The emotion I determine in him, with scarcely a word or gesture to illustrate it, is proud and ardent love for you. Bingley, who knows him so well, believes... "

Kitty's entrance at that moment was most unwelcome to Elizabeth, but she tried, with less success than Jane, to give a warm welcome to a sister conscious of neglect. It was always easier to succeed with Georgiana, who dearly loved Elizabeth, was unconsciously jealous of Jane and increasingly critical of the contrived compliments offered by her friend, Miss Bingley.

The dinner party provided a flurry of activity with the young adults enjoying an impromptu dance. Even Georgiana had to join in, being unable to retreat to the piano as none of her music was appropriate. The local guests left after breakfast the following morning, followed by the Bennets and the Bingleys at the end of the week.

When all the guests had departed, Elizabeth firmly led Darcy to the library, where they could discuss her conversation with Mrs Reynolds in more business-like surroundings than the conjugal bed.

"Beloved husband, recently I have been talking to – you might say, consulting with – Mrs Reynolds about the charitable activities traditionally performed by the wives of Pemberley. She emphasised the fact that your mother's role was limited by ill health, but while I am capable of more, and anxious to do more, I would like to include a wider involvement than the Schools. Mr Warriner is so indecisive he needs a wife to organize him, ideally a woman deeply concerned with both catechism and needlework as I am poorly qualified to work in these areas!"

"I totally agree. Your primary talents do not lie in those directions! But I fear Warriner may not be a marrying man, so different solutions must be sought. But I would like to explain more about my mother; other than charitable contributions, annual prize givings at the Schools were almost the full extent of her involvement. Not only was her health poor, but her nature was too aloof for personal contacts. I acknowledge the same trait…"

His wife interrupted with a warm defence, but Darcy had referred to his mother in connection with present anxieties about his sister.

"It is about Georgiana that I am concerned. Since my father's death she has become increasingly shy and reserved, even with me, for I lack my father's open nature. I do believe she understands how dearly I love her, but she is visibly happier now you are here. Incomparable Elizabeth, this comes as no surprise to me – how could it possibly be? But perhaps you can render her even greater help. Georgiana has little of the dominant family pride of which my mother and I may be accused, yet most unfortunately is perceived to have a great deal. In appearance she is now so mature and dignified, that no stranger would realise she is five years your junior, and casual acquaintances mistakenly believe her reserved air is produced by a sense of superiority, rather than timidity.

"Sadly, the episode with Wickham increased her general insecurity. It must be remembered that she was not only deceived by him, but by her chaperon, Mrs Younge, who accepted almost the position of a mother only to abuse that trust. It is reassuring to observe that her new companion, Mrs Annesley, has repaired some of that damage, but she belongs particularly to London life and is not always at Pemberley."

Here Darcy paused, fearing that Elizabeth would accept the following request without consulting her own inclinations. Wanting her to be free to express doubts, he tried to disguise the serious nature of his hopes by repeating her joke about the reasons for Warriner needing a wife.

"Georgiana is fond of small children but afraid of becoming a Visitor at the Schools. If Warriner disobligingly remains unmarried despite your amiable plans on his behalf, perhaps you might see your way to begin working with Georgiana in the youngest class of girls, leaving her to continue on her own once she felt at ease?"

These affectionate intentions failed, for Elizabeth successfully concealed her sense of inadequacy behind a willing offer of help. This apparently brought the conversation to an end, until on a sudden impulse she stood on a library step – not to reach a book, but to bring her eyes on a level with his – and entirely surprised her husband by voicing her feelings about their lack of privacy.

"Lack of privacy, beautiful and adored Elizabeth?"

She laughed and blushed.

"I do not mean lack of privacy in our bedchamber but the total change from private to public life the moment we leave it. When can I do *this* during the day? Look at you in this way, laugh with you, hold your hand? I find it inhibiting to have servants ever in attendance; not actively occupied, but just waiting for orders."

She added hastily, and with almost total honesty,

"I do not at all include Georgiana in these comments about privacy. I think she would not be displeased, would almost certainly like it, if I was sometimes frivolous and teasing, and if we felt free to show our affection. No, not like that. I only wish to take your hand, or have your arm round me."

"It is hard to restrain myself when you stand so close, but it is also true that my upbringing emphasised formality. Somehow the atmosphere of Pemberley makes it natural for me to keep my feelings under control until we are alone at night."

Natural and *correct*, more accurately described his attitude to the stately routines of Pemberley that seemed as much a part of the house as the stones from which it was constructed. He explained that the household provided training for local boys and girls who then found employment elsewhere, it was therefore a service provided by the Darcys rather than for the Darcys and consequently not easy to change. Half jesting, he asked, "Surely the courage that I have seen rise to every challenge will not be subdued by some supernumerary footmen?"

"It is a constraint rather than a challenge; at Pemberley I have no adversaries. Perhaps that is the problem: I am surrounded by kindness." She looked rather than spoke her feelings before continuing. "But there must be time to make fun of the small follies of daily life, and be playful with my husband - even if Lady Catherine believes this pollutes the shades of Pemberley."

"You brighten what Lady Catherine chose to call *'the shades of Pemberley'*. Think how much Georgiana's happiness has grown in your company. As for me, your lively wit attracted me as much as your beautiful eyes. And since our marriage I have been so deeply moved... behind that beguiling manner lies such strength of feeling. If you are uneasy because your playful spirits have been briefly suppressed, be assured their return is inevitable for the compelling reason that they are true to your serious emotions despite the seeming contrast."

"Dear Darcy, your judgement is temporarily clouded by affection, but in the future I mean to be wise as well as merry. I was needlessly impertinent to you in those early encounters when I used mockery to sooth my vanity."

"*My* vanity has decided that we were both instinctively drawn to each other; what you call impertinence appeared to me (and not only to me) an attractive challenge. Unfortunately my argument is somewhat weakened by the fact that I have never seen any man affronted by your wit."

"I think so well of your argument that I am firmly persuaded of it, unless this requires me to be in love with everyone I tease."

"Certainly not."

The conclusion to this conversation was so pleasing that Elizabeth was content that at least the question of footmen had been raised, if not conclusively settled.

Her impulsive action had been ill timed considering that the Earl and Countess of Otterburn (the senior members of the Fitzwilliam family) would arrive tomorrow. Obviously they would know of her family background, but fortunately for Elizabeth's peace of mind, she was unaware that their informant was her old enemy, Lady Catherine de Bourgh. With angry detail they had been assured the girl was impertinent; the father only minor gentry; the mother ill bred and ignorant; and one of the sisters scandalously involved with the disgraced son of a Pemberley retainer.

Although Augustus Fitzwilliam was sensible that his nephew (whose wealth was greater than his own) need consult no one about his marriage, nevertheless, as head of the family the news had displeased him. By birth this young woman, whatever her attractions, belonged to a class that should have placed her completely outside Darcy's sphere. She was surely too lowborn to be his wife and too respectable to be his mistress. Becoming infatuated enough to marry her was a grave miscalculation. A notorious womaniser himself, the Earl understood all these nuances and had always abided by them. Therefore his congratulatory letter was almost curt, but he did not intend this marriage to affect the winter visit he and his Countess usually made to Derbyshire en route for London and the south. He had caused no family quarrel and the deplorable wife would be treated to a carefully measured degree of civility.

Darcy was not unaware of all this, but relying on the fact that his wife would have no basis for comparison, merely offered this warning: "My uncle is somewhat uneven in temper – precisely the reverse of his son, Colonel Fitzwilliam, who greatly enjoyed making your acquaintance at Rosings last spring. *His* behaviour, even in less felicitous circumstances, is always easy and pleasant, whereas his father, the Earl, can vary noticeably between jovial and morose, and the Countess, an admirable and learned woman, has manners some people consider eccentric. Otterburn is far more isolated than Pemberley and those bleak moors are subject to fiercer winters than you are ever likely to experience here. Consequently, my aunt and uncle travel south at this time of year in search of distractions, taking Pemberley in on the way."

It did not suit Elizabeth's pride to ask Darcy if (as she half suspected) her presence might make the Earl morose, but she did apply to Georgiana for further general information about the Fitzwilliams of Otterburn. A somewhat unsatisfactory conversation ensued, both young ladies having a number of thoughts they wished to leave unspoken.

"As your aunt and uncle are entire strangers to me, perhaps you can give me your ideas of what to expect?"

"My aunt is so learned and authoritative that as a child I was rather frightened of her." This was said hesitantly enough to suggest the fear was not entirely in the past.

"Like your other aunt, Lady Catherine de Bourgh?"

"No, not at all, but how hard it is to describe family members accepted from childhood days without question. My two aunts are both confident characters, but alike in little else. Aunt Henrietta is inclined to silence, and rarely makes personal remarks about people. When I consider her objectively (rather than as an older relation I have known all my life) she is enthusiastic about all manner of subjects such a literature, art, history, but displays a limited interest in the society around her. She resembles my brother in being extremely well-informed over a wide range of topics – but her way of speaking is not like his either; both are admirable in different ways, so I must leave you to judge for yourself. As for my uncle, my view is too much coloured by my childhood sense of inadequacy in his company. Much of his time is spent in the highest society and he naturally expects his niece, almost seventeen years old, to be composed and confidant. Even now, when I should do better, I feel awkward in his company. However, you will have nothing to fear in that regard."

Then unhappily remembering the Earl's contempt for people of less consequence than himself, a sense of duty obliged her to mention that this uncle was perhaps too aware of rank, especially his title and the eminence of his wife's family. Lacking Georgiana's timidity, Elizabeth did not mean to be alarmed by the Earl, and while noting that his wife's company might be a challenge, turned the conversation to their younger son.

"You know I have the pleasure of being acquainted with Colonel Fitzwilliam, but your comments, added to your brother's, suggest that in manner there is little resemblance between him and his parents, though his knowledge of books and music (of which we mainly spoke together) may come from his mother."

Elizabeth spoke lightly, concealing the fact that the Colonel had paid her marked attention at Rosings, while scrupulously making it clear that he could not afford to marry a dowerless woman. She had found him a thoroughly agreeable man, and not more mercenary than his circumstances demanded. He had demonstrated none of the excessive pride manifested in different ways by both his aunt and his cousin Darcy. It seemed that the Fitzwilliam hauteur (apparently epitomised by his father, the Earl) had no part in his nature. Indeed during that period of bad judgement Elizabeth had thought him equal to Wickham in charm of address and conversation, and infinitely superior to his cousin. She had learned to love Darcy and despise Wickham but hoped to retain her affectionate regard for Colonel Fitzwilliam.

Georgiana chose to say little about him, for she too had feelings to conceal. Her cousin was also her guardian (sharing that responsibility with her brother) and she had enjoyed years of kind solicitude. Now she was ashamed that he knew all about her infatuation with George Wickham, for by sheer mischance he understood more than her brother. One day, finding her struggling with an agony of tears, he somehow recognised that her feelings involved intense physical passion as well as girlish adoration. It was so shaming that, if her upright nature could be guilty of such selfishness, she would have rejoiced that the war with France kept him abroad.

The Otterburns arrived well before dinner. First impressions showed the Earl to be a man of middle height, stiff deportment and inexpressive features. His wife was more striking, being positively plain and ungainly, with a careless style of dress that did nothing to compensate for these disadvantages. Elizabeth looked forward to studying her character. Lord Otterburn, expecting from his sister's information a vividly assertive young woman, had assumed a voluptuous figure and outstanding beauty of feature. This girl was slighter than Georgiana and looked scarcely older - was certainly pretty, but nothing exceptional, in fact her figure and general manner did not entirely satisfy his standards.

Seated by her at dinner he offered, in a correct but unenthusiastic way, the compliments due to a bride, which she accepted calmly before leading him into a more general conversation. With some irritation he noticed that his niece had not outgrown her childish state of tongue-tied nerves, while this Miss Nobody was quite at her ease asking him pertinent questions about his visit to a venerable, but long-neglected, mansion in the neighbourhood.

"My wife's connections you know; in some way or other she is related to most of the grand old families. You will have to ask her to explain about it being empty and unoccupied now. I am sometimes inclined to do that with Otterburn; ruinously expensive and uncomfortable to live in are these medieval structures despite their grandeur. Darcy has it relatively easy here, Pemberley is a goodish size but it does not sprawl over the landscape like the really ancient places."

"In my eyes Pemberley has every beauty, including grandeur," said Elizabeth with a smile, "and I am amazed to find it also enjoys the comforts of running water piped to many rooms. My old home, which is so much smaller, has none. Of course there is still the problem of heating the water for baths, but I think it a great advantage that servants have fewer heavy cans to carry up and down stairs."

She could hardly allude to the other great benefit - an ingenious system of water closets. Even without that solecism the Earl thought her concern for servants thoroughly bourgeois. Darcy could hear his uncle instructing Elizabeth about the streams flowing from the moors above Pemberley making piped water feasible, to which she listened courteously without disclosing that she was already well-informed on this subject, including new plans for using hot water pipes to provide some heat to passageways and reception rooms. Thinking of this very topic, Darcy turned to his aunt, apologising for Pemberley's cold corridors, to which she replied,

"You very well know they are an improvement on Otterburn, but I haven't hesitated to wear my woollen pelisse for the journey from bedchamber to dining-parlour." She leaned over to address her niece. "Georgiana, you and Mrs Darcy should follow my example; men are always dressed warmly, yet expect women to remain scarcely covered."

"But Aunt, my brother has given us both these wonderfully large Indian shawls. I assure you he is always most careful of our comfort."

The Countess had good-naturedly made this remark knowing her niece would be stirred to speak in defence of her beloved brother, however, when Georgiana lapsed into silence she made no further effort. Henrietta Fitzwilliam was almost ten years her husband's senior, having brought neither beauty nor money to the marriage. She rarely spoke of family connections, leaving that to her husband - who enjoyed drawing attention to them. In her quixotic view, plain country gentry were often preferable to recently created baronets and viscounts; this new Mrs Darcy was the daughter of a gentleman, and though the mother's family could never be acceptable, she was willing to wait and see what the girl herself was like. As for the younger Bennet sister, obviously she was disgraced by her patched-up marriage weeks after an elopement, but the Countess was used to libertines and adulterers; her husband was one, and so was her elder son - it was to be hoped his heir (if he ever had one) would take after some other members of the family. Better still if Henry, the younger son, succeeded his brother, but it was imperative he find a wife with money in addition to good blood. She could not work up much righteous indignation about Lydia Bennet, other than her choosing someone as low-born as George Wickham. Of Georgiana's earlier entanglement with Wickham, she knew nothing. The secret had been well kept by Colonel Fitzwilliam despite the warm attachment between mother and son.

As the week passed, Elizabeth developed a better understanding of Lady Otterburn. Although her rather forbidding appearance was not softened by conciliating manners, hostility was not the cause. It was refreshing to be with someone so totally unselfconscious. Silent as often as not, when she did speak, mundane topics would be given a fresh slant, or an unusual piece of information offered. Initially Elizabeth feared she was to meet an older version of her pedantic sister, Mary, but here a great fund of knowledge was expressed in a straightforward, sensible, way.

From further observation of the Otterburns, Elizabeth concluded that in this uncompanionable marriage the wife found compensation in intellectual pursuits - and was strangely moved by this similarity to her own father's life. Suggesting this to her husband, he instinctively disagreed, but managed to stop short of complaining that it came unsuitably close to comparing the Earl of Otterburn with Mrs Bennet. His uncle stripped of the attributes of rank had not much to commend him, but he wasn't complacently ignorant and vulgar... then honesty forced him to admit that Otterburn's ignorance was complacent - but that only emphasised the vast gulf between good breeding and bad. He kept these thoughts from his wife, but she was reaching a similar conclusion. Her mother's dislike of Darcy had been vulgarly demonstrated in company, while Lord Otterburn, who probably felt an even stronger distaste for his nephew's new wife, never deviated from formal politeness. Even so, Elizabeth could not think well of the Earl whose pride of birth seemed divorced from any sense of duty; it might almost be claimed that Lady Catherine's outrageous interference in the lives of all around her was preferable.

As the Otterburns were not musical their hosts accepted a request for some reading after dinner. The Earl only participated by listening, but Darcy was so effective with a selection of the King's speeches in Henry IV that the ladies longed for more. The following morning, when the three of them sat together, some scenes from *As You Like It* were suggested; Georgiana found courage to express doubt: "Mrs Annesley thinks it an unsuitable play; I believe my brother agrees with that, and so I am not sure..."

"Why is that I wonder?" enquired Elizabeth, reluctant to have her husband limit her reading, and therefore continuing with, "It is one of the few plays I have seen performed, and other than thinking the second half too longwinded it was such a charming pastoral."

"I had forgotten the delicate way girls are raised these days." said the Countess. "I was near fifty when you were born, Georgiana, and my upbringing was much more robust. Shakespeare is full of sex, comically earthy as well as seriously passionate, because life is like that. I imagine that Darcy (at least in the family circle) would be happy to play Orlando to his wife's Rosalind, but reluctant to have his sister read Celia. In your innocent girlhood, Mrs Darcy, you probably missed most of the crude jokes and sexual word-play, but now you have a husband to inform you of things a brother may be in no hurry to tell his sister."

Elizabeth made no response to this assessment of her husband, merely replying, "That explains why I found some parts boring and obscure. In your company I learn something new every day. I wish you were not leaving so soon, unless you can encourage me to hope for conversation at Huntleigh equal to this?"

"I am delighted that we go together to Huntleigh, but I am afraid the conversation will be very dull, although they are the best of people, and Theodora my oldest friend. Whatever persuaded her husband to think himself elevated by becoming the first Lord Ridgeway I shall never understand; they have been the Hunts of Huntleigh for seven hundred years, how can you improve on that? Mind you, some changes can be for the better; decades ago they built a new Palladian house which offers comfortable living space in addition to the splendid reception rooms where a ball will be given in your honour. You, Mrs Darcy, will endure all the tedium of being welcomed as the new bride, and I shall be happy to follow you in to dinner and drink your health."

Lady Otterburn had found more pleasure at Pemberley than she expected. Georgiana's wearying diffidence became less apparent every day, and Darcy's newly acquired wife was a lively girl, intelligent and unpretentious. She would probably be a good thing for both Darcy and his sister, assuming her family was kept at a distance. By contrast, her husband's visit had been less enjoyable. Although the newly married couple were not demonstrative in public, nothing could disguise the happiness of mutual passion. The Earl responded by finding Elizabeth increasingly attractive, while still considering her an unworthy consort for Darcy. That naturally sparkling manner seemed to him an unfair tease, yet Henrietta, uncharacteristically, favoured the girl. It seemed the final annoyance that they were all going to visit Huntleigh where his wife would have to give precedence to the bride.

Elizabeth made her first public appearance as Mrs Darcy at a ball in one of the most elegant houses in England. Lord Ridgeway, having received adverse reports, found Mrs Darcy agreeably conversible at dinner the first day, and helpfully light on her feet when led out to open the dancing the following night. Lady Ridgeway judged her not demure enough for a bride, but gave her credit for gaining Henrietta Fitzwilliam's strong approval. This encounter with Darcy's wife relieved the worst anxieties of the Ridgeways. Other than the Otterburn connection there was no intimate friendship between the two families, but it was essential for the great landowners to remain on good terms. By attending a ball in her honour the landed gentry of Derbyshire and its neighbouring counties, paid their respects to the new Mrs Darcy, whose captivating appearance caused her husband to enjoy the occasion almost as much as she did - and Elizabeth dearly loved to dance.

    The moment of greatest happiness arrived when they found themselves together in that same dance in which they had been partners more than a year ago. Determinedly prejudiced against him then, Elizabeth knew she had been insolent rather than playful. Somewhat ashamed at the time, her recollections grew ever more painful as she gradually learned to understand his character. Now chance offered her the perfect moment to erase those memories. But even as she began to apologise, Darcy repeated some of those provocative comments, demanding her help to recall others. The occasion had drawn him deeper into love, however reluctant he had been to admit it at the time.

When Elizabeth was not present, the ladies' conversation had more bite and malice. The girl had dressed cleverly for the occasion wearing that priceless lace over a simple gown and with the family pearls in her hair. But when Darcy decided against his sickly cousin, why had he selected someone with such odious connections? His choice was felt as a general insult, and one or two of the younger ladies present took it as a personal insult. All the families had known each other for generations and although Darcy, like his father before him, was not considered a seriously dedicated sportsman, the continuing prosperity of his estate attested to his knowledge as much as his wealth. It displayed uncharacteristically poor judgement to marry a woman who knew nothing about the county and had no place in Society. However, Georgiana, with her desirable thirty thousand pounds, was spending an increasing amount of time with her newly married brother, so his wife must not be completely snubbed.

To Georgiana it was impossible that any fault should be found with either her brother or sister, and to some degree Darcy's pride subscribed to the same conviction. If he recognised courtesy rather than warmth, it was all he wanted from these particular neighbours. Elizabeth, perhaps the sharpest observer on this occasion, knew that at Huntleigh she had failed to impress the women, but saw no need to force herself into the conventional mode. She would gradually become accepted.

Judging the whole party, other than Lady Otterburn, to offer no more interest than the inhabitants of Meryton, Elizabeth was very ready to return to Pemberley where she would be making her formal appearance as Mrs Darcy at a dinner given to all the tenant farmers and their wives. In its way this would be a greater challenge, but she suspected it might be crowned with greater success.

✍ Scene Four ✍

The Darcys were to leave for London soon after the tenants' party, so it was fortunate for Elizabeth that all the arrangements for food and entertainment were in Mrs Reynold's capable hands.

As mid-winter was not the usual season for this celebration, it was, of necessity, held in the Long Gallery instead of the tithe barn. With the open fireplaces merely creating islands of warmth amid the prevailing cold, warm dress was recommended, but as often happens with good advice, many of the younger women chose to ignore it. Decisions, based purely on vanity, fortunately proved justified when the dancing started and the temperature rose.

Some of the people were already known to Elizabeth - Farmer Webb, her first partner, belonged to a family who had been on Darcy lands for centuries, and proved surprisingly light on his feet despite a back bent by a lifetime of work on a moorland farm. He attended to Elizabeth with a hearty good will that seemed paternal rather than deferential. Her next partner, Mr Biggs, was a complete contrast, a young man farming prosperous valley acres - in manner entirely the gentleman. Being fatherless he was head of a family consisting of his mother, a younger brother who was learning farm management from him, and two sisters both attending a Seminary in Bath, the elder almost finished, and a shy younger girl whose silence was noticeable among that agreeably friendly family. When her dance with Mr Biggs was over she was surprised to learn that he had not met Miss Darcy for many years now. Seeing Georgiana stiffly silent beside Mrs Reynolds, she reintroduced him and, having performed the ceremony, watched complacently as they joined the dance, only to receive an unwelcome hint from Mrs Reynolds and a severe look from her husband. She assumed it was some nonsensical difference made between Mr Darcy's wife, who could be safely partnered by any tenant, and his eligible sister who should avoid dancing with a bachelor farmer judged to be on the borderlines of gentility. Elizabeth meant to challenge this later, but, as she watched her husband during the next few hours, her resentment diminished.

The stately manner that caused offence at Meryton, seemed here to proclaim duty and responsibility rather than privilege. Like his father before him, Darcy was a knowledgeable and considerate landlord, and the respect shown by the tenants was far from the puerile servility of a Mr Collins. Elizabeth, admiring these relationships, felt she had not yet earned the right to criticise, although she continued to think her husband and Mrs Reynolds wrong in their attitude to young Farmer Biggs. That Georgiana had seemed to enjoy dancing with him and being re-introduced to his family may have been the root of the trouble. However, change was inevitable; to a certain degree she herself was an example.

The familiar route to London was to be varied this time, creating some resistance from the head coachman, who remained in overall charge however many teams of post horses were brought into use. Darcy made this rearrangement on behalf of his wife, knowing that while Georgiana could sit passively for a long morning Elizabeth's active nature disliked the confinement of a closed carriage. He confessed that as Wilson talked of exertion and rest in connection with horses, his mind was occupied with similar thoughts about her. Hearing his words to Elizabeth, Georgiana was surprised to find her brother could be jocular.

"Can you forgive me, that for a moment you and the horses were confused in my mind? I had to pause before continuing the discussion with Wilson."

"I am not sure I am willing to be one of four matched horses," laughed Elizabeth, "or worse still, an odd lot from a livery stable. On the other hand, a comparison with my mare would be almost too flattering, her nature undoubtedly being more obedient than mine, not to mention those limpid eyes and six inch long eyelashes."

As they were both well aware of his particular admiration for her brightly expressive eyes, Darcy gravely offered the following observation. "But I possibly prefer the size, colour, and general distribution of your teeth."

Details of their journey were explained. This husbandly solicitude was perhaps excessive, but Elizabeth had no fault to find with it. Following these new plans they started early on the first day, stopping before noon to visit a friend of his. The parish of Kympton, originally intended for Wickham, had for two years been in the charge of Mr Gervase, Darcy's ex-tutor. A young and erudite scholar, apparently fully absorbed by the masculine life of an Oxford college, he had been increasingly preoccupied by the need to care for his invalid mother, until the offer of Kympton provided a happy solution to his problem while giving Darcy the pleasure of settling a valued friend within easy reach of Pemberley. But Gervase had surprised everyone by marrying soon after he resigned his Fellowship; there was already an infant daughter to whom Darcy was to be godfather.

The travellers were given a warm welcome by Mr Gervase, who was everything that Elizabeth expected, followed by his wife, who looked almost too young to be the mother of the baby in her arms. There had been a hint of deference in Darcy's manner to his admired tutor, but the intent look he turned on Mrs Gervase was grave, even though accompanied by formal courtesies. He worried that his friend, inexperienced in the ways of women, had too quickly succumbed to childish prettiness. There were additionally discouraging facts: Mrs Gervase had been a governess, and still worse, the family for whom she had worked were only moderately genteel. The marriage meant great advancement for her, but would Gervase be happy in it? From his own point of view Darcy saw only disadvantages. Visits between Pemberley and Kympton would either be hurried matters of business or elaborate family affairs involving a wife whose only concerns would presumably be her children. As Mrs Gervase and Georgiana remained indoors while the others walked in the shrubbery, there was no opportunity to test this assumption, for the group who assembled in the dining-parlour for refreshments proved too large for uninterrupted conversation. Not only did the elderly mother of Gervase make her appearance, but also two young sisters of Mrs Gervase.

They resumed their journey with Georgiana as unusually talkative as Elizabeth was silent.

"Mrs Gervase and her child were delightful; I was allowed to carry the baby when we went out to the kitchen to see that everything was ready. I was surprised when her younger sisters suggested I call them Bella and Maria, and initially supposed they were still young enough for that." Trying to ignore a lack of enthusiasm in her brother, she added, "Fitzwilliam, can you credit that they are really as old as sixteen and eighteen? Shall we see them all at Pemberley? They were so agreeable that I felt entirely at ease, especially as in that busy household it was remarkable they had any time to spare for me."

Darcy admitted to himself that his friend seemed genuinely fond of his young sisters-in-law, who closely resembled his wife while lacking her pretty features. Assuredly a man happy as husband and brother deserved his warmest approval. And remembering his tender way with the baby, Darcy's gaze rested thoughtfully on his own wife as he contemplated the future. She was less responsive than usual when Georgiana (taken aback by her silence) pressed for an opinion. Elizabeth's personal reflections were painful but she exerted herself to appear composed, having no wish to draw attention to unhappy similarities between the three Porter sisters and the Bennet family.

There had been a frightening lack of security for those unmarried girls before Mr Gervase welcomed them into his home. But her own father, by an early death, might have left his daughters even less secure; at least the Misses Porter had always known they must be prepared to teach. For selfish reasons Elizabeth was heartily glad that Mr Bennet of Longbourn, a gentleman of independent means, could not have his daughters trained up as governesses, but how improvident that no savings were ever made from his comfortable income. Something so essential to the security of his family should certainly have been done from the beginning of his marriage.

Even the thwarted plan to break the entail with the help of a son, would had meant impoverishing his heir (and all following descendents) to avoid making economies in his own lifetime. If fundamentally the cause was indolence rather than selfishness, nevertheless it remained inexcusable that her father joked about the penurious situation of his survivors when Mr Collins inherited the estate. Elizabeth reluctantly admitted that her mother's vulgar pursuit of husbands for her daughters at least showed appropriate concern. Turning her face away from the window, she answered questions about the Gervase family as briefly as possible, before directing Georgiana's attention to a change in the scenery.

Several more stages, followed by poor lodgings, provided enough reasons for them all to be tired and out of spirits. The bed provided for man and wife was so intolerably lumpy that Darcy retreated to a narrow, equally lumpy, mattress in the dressing room. The Inn Keeper was rebuked, but Elizabeth was grateful for a night alone to compose her feelings. Her thoughts ran on a conversation with Jane just after she had accepted Bingley.

'Lizzy if there were but such another man for you.' followed by her own comment, *'Until I have your disposition, your goodness, I can never have your happiness.'* Then the joke she could not resist, *'If I have very good luck I may meet another Mr Collins in time.'*

Of course she would never have accepted anyone so conceited and silly, but as the years pressed on, would she have been forced to lower her high expectations? It was against all odds that she had attracted a man such as Fitzwilliam Darcy or that his love had survived her determined prejudice.

A night of restless dreams was broken early next morning by a maid struggling with the fire, so Elizabeth, washing and dressing quickly, went down to the forecourt of the Inn and successfully distracted her thoughts by watching the activity generated by horses, coaches, ostlers, and travellers. Darcy, seeing this from the dressing room window, wished his wife would remember the need to be properly accompanied but decided not to mention his disapproval. He decided not to mention the Gervase family either, but Elizabeth forestalled him by saying at breakfast: "I am glad Kympton is near enough to exchange visits. You already have your friend, and Georgiana and I hope to see more of Mrs Gervase and her sisters."

She had recovered most of her spirits and was looking forward to London attractions while her husband remained gloomily preoccupied. His wife envied his freedom to ride some stages on horseback, without fully realising that the purpose was not only to enjoy fresh air and exercise but also to avoid conversation. Unfortunately, even the benefits bestowed by physical exertion and uninterrupted thought could not totally dispel Darcy's mood.

Elizabeth's rejection of his first offer of marriage had brought about months of painful self-evaluation. Although won over to unqualified regard for those whose natural qualities were of high order – his dear wife, her sister, aunt, and uncle - he still believed in the claims of birth. He observed good sense and good principles in Mrs Gervase, but she and her sisters were not well bred; their lack of artifice (in general, much to be commended) made a certain homeliness of manner uncomfortably apparent. A wife must share her husband's rank, but that certainly need not apply to all her relations; it was therefore unfortunate that Georgiana particularly wished the sisters to be invited to Pemberley, and that Elizabeth repeated the suggestion this morning. In Darcy's estimation the condition in life of those girls was closer to that of his trusted old friend Mrs Reynolds. Had it not been for their connection with

Gervase they would more properly be entertained in the housekeeper's room.

Perhaps the distractions of London would make the family at Kympton recede into the background. Georgiana would return to her own establishment, presided over by Mrs Annesley, a woman of unassailable good breeding, whose chief task was to ensure that Georgiana made a wide acquaintance among suitable young people. Of course she would often be with her brother and sister, but with Elizabeth making her debut in Society it hardly seemed appropriate for her to act as chaperon, particularly as the Bingleys would be their guests.

For Darcy, high hopes for this London Season were modified by fears that an episode from the previous season might prove an embarrassment. At this time last year, Bingley had been a guest in his house, innocent of the extent of his host's determination to keep him from Jane Bennet. While Bingley's feelings for the eldest Bennet girl were dangerously apparent, Darcy strove to suppress his passionate response to the younger sister. The two young men busied themselves with all the available pleasures and distractions, making Darcy particularly susceptible to an amorous relationship that seemed to require no great intensity or commitment. The lady in question, was a widow ten or fifteen years his senior, beautiful, well born, highly educated. Inevitably their families had numerous mutual friends although she and Darcy had hitherto met infrequently. Gossip chose to assume she must have taken lovers among the unattached men who sought her company in the years following her husband's death, but unlike the women who had first encouraged Darcy's attentions, she was both discreet and far from promiscuous. In the natural course of events their friendship would have survived the end of the affair. Transient as they both knew the affair must be, his mistress, though strongly attached to him, considered it her right to choose the moment at which to end it.

Unfortunately Darcy's feelings changed abruptly after unexpectedly spending three weeks as the near neighbour of Elizabeth Bennet. He had hoped he was distancing himself from this entrancing, but unsuitable, young woman, but once restored to her company, his feelings intensified. Fully confident of being accepted, he confessed the irresistible force of his love, only to find himself rejected in the most mortifying terms.

Darcy had returned to London in even greater need of consolation, but with his affections utterly committed to Elizabeth any other relationship was impossible. Unfortunately his mistress had genuinely loved him; consequently, she was not only distressed, but also affronted by this ruthless break.

Now almost a year had passed. She would know of his recent marriage and they should be able to meet with the appearance of ease, but *he* would not be easy. If it were not an inexcusable discourtesy he would really prefer to discontinue the acquaintance.

Despite this lingering difficulty, Darcy enjoyed introducing Elizabeth to London Society. As Charles Bingley was even more uxorious than Darcy, the men's shared activities did not often extend beyond occasions when their wives were busy with dressmakers or events for ladies only. The wives chosen by two such eligible bachelors - for Bingley's pleasing address and general sensibility almost compensated for his less elevated birth and fortune - were bound to be objects of interest. London society duly scrutinized them, and after the Darcys and the Bingleys had given several formal receptions the Bennet sisters were discovered to be sufficiently handsome, agreeable and conversible, even if a few disappointed young ladies decided that Mrs Bingley's beauty was insipid, and Mrs Darcy's appearance not outstanding enough to warrant the air of cheerful assurance with which she was making her first appearance in High Society.

Fortunately the general view was not quite so severe. Despite their low connections, Jane rose steadily in the estimation of all while Elizabeth received a more varied report. Making their debut at Almack's Club, where seven titled 'patronesses' strictly controlled admission, the number of members attracted by Mrs Darcy's liveliness was balanced by those who pronounced that same manner unacceptable in the fashionable world.

When Charles Bingley introduced Elizabeth to a group of his friends she was covertly scrutinised by a Mrs Cartwright, the doyenne of a lively and well-informed group of friends with interests extending beyond the essentially trivial boundaries of Almack's. When everyone had exchanged the proper courtesies, Mrs Cartwright disengaged herself from the general conversation to address Elizabeth.

"Now here is a question which has been creating great excitement amongst us. No sooner has the quadrille been granted respectability by Almack's arbiters of taste, than the possibility of the waltz is under consideration. What do you think, Mrs Darcy? Can the decorous spirit of this club survive?"

"This being my first visit, I cannot answer for Almack's, but for myself, I have rarely waltzed and would welcome any occasion to do so. From Mrs Cartwright's smile and tone of voice I think she may share my belief that a particularly nice attention to decorum is often the province of those who find themselves no longer able to enjoy innocent amusements, and consequently wish to deny them to others. Why should more cheerful spirits be deprived of a pleasure already available to respectable society in several of the capital cities of Europe, apparently with no devastating effect on the moral structure of those nations? And to include a crudely practical argument, in this long cold winter it is a wonderful way of keeping warm."

"Bravely spoken, Mrs Darcy. Now I am certain of your approbation I dare confess that I have enjoyed waltzing in Vienna and hope to waltz here in due course. But what are your husband's views? I believe I heard he is not fond of dancing, unless you have won him over?"

Unaware that the opening words of this apparently innocuous question were disingenuous, Elizabeth suggested, "He must speak for himself – if the question is not already answered by the fact that even now he is coming down the dance with my sister, Mrs Bingley."

Then, turning to her brother-in-law, "Charles! I believe you might be able to attract their attention for a moment when they come to a pause?"

The movements of the quadrille insured it was indeed a brief encounter, for Darcy, although close to them, was not facing in their direction. When Bingley tapped him on the shoulder, hurried bows were exchanged without audible words, and when the dance ended, the Darcys joined a different group of people for the remainder of the evening. Elizabeth regretted the change.

Fitzwilliam Darcy by nature and education was well equipped to instruct, and his wife was very ready to be instructed. He increased her knowledge of London's history and architecture, visited the booksellers with her, took her to the play, and most importantly, to hear music performed on a grander scale than she had ever encountered before. For this last experience her natural taste was on a higher level than his - as he readily conceded. In the visual arts they both accepted Lady Otterburn as their guide, for Darcy was increasingly aware that the Long Gallery at Pemberley contained too few paintings of note in its daunting length. The canvases were mediocre compared with the quality of the collection of books in the library, lovingly assembled over generations. With marriage bringing thoughts of new portraits, he visited the Royal Academy with his wife, but his aunt soon educated them to think not only of portraits but of serious investment in seventeenth and eighteenth century paintings, a study newly attractive to Elizabeth, who had hitherto concerned herself only with faithful representations of people or scenery.

Encouraged by Mrs Annesley, Georgiana was formally 'At Home' one afternoon a week, and relied upon Elizabeth to come as frequently as possible. It was there she encountered Mrs Cartwright's son: a very young man, but not the schoolboy she had expected considering his mother's relatively youthful appearance. He was plain in face and figure, but his conversation was as apt and engaging as his mother's and within a short space of time he had not only described his work - examining and cataloguing private art collections – but invited Miss Darcy and Mrs Darcy to join him and his mother at Mr Fawkes' home in Grosvenor Place where watercolour landscapes by J M W Turner were on view.

That the visit was a great success did not depend solely upon the watercolours. The group (which included Jane) were so easy and pleasant with each other, far beyond the lifeless formality common to many of their new acquaintances. Mrs Cartwright remained almost the only interesting woman to make overtures of friendship to Elizabeth, although Jane (faring somewhat better) urged that probably the young women they met were sensible and agreeable among themselves even if rather reserved with newcomers. No doubt by next season they would be welcome. Elizabeth chose to conceal her opinion that the Bennet sisters were unwelcome because they had removed two eligible bachelors from a London Season chronically handicapped by a surplus of women.

She imagined some unflattering comments. *"Mrs Bingley might almost be forgiven because her qualities were so outstanding, but that Mrs Darcy..."* Despising their paltry motives, her courage rose in self-defence, but she also recognised that, within reason, the women who were married to Darcy's friends must become her friends. She decided to agree with Jane that by next season – or the following one - they would be comfortably assimilated.

The second reason for the success of this visit was entirely due to J M W Turner. His work was already familiar through etchings, or large oil paintings of historical or mythological subjects, but the watercolours introduced a new world of delight, making Elizabeth determined to buy one as a gift to the husband who so generously lavished presents upon her. The choice presented some agreeable difficulties. Several return visits were made, usually in the company of Georgiana and the knowledgeable Mr Cartwright, but without his mother. Elizabeth appreciated Mrs Cartwright's instinctive delicacy in understanding that *her* advice - someone whose connection with the Darcy family was distant though long established – would not be relevant. With some regret Elizabeth suspected her husband preferred to maintain this distance while she herself would have enjoyed an increasing intimacy.

Darcy had been away with Bingley, helping him conclude the purchase of Dufton Hall, a rapid fulfilment (true to Charles' impetuous nature) of plans discussed with the Darcys soon after Christmas. A mere thirty miles south of Pemberley, the park reflected the soft contours of the countryside, and the house itself, of fairly recent date, was both handsome and comfortable. Furniture belonging to the Bingley family had already arrived, and although more would be needed they were in no hurry as long as a reasonable number of the rooms were finished - including nurseries, for Jane hoped she was already expecting a child.

Most understandably they wished to complete the move in the next month or two, making Elizabeth feel how well everything was settled. Her own wishes were now inclined to a slow approach towards making changes at Pemberley, while Jane was ideally suited to creating a new home. The Darcys were to be the first visitors at Dufton Hall once they had fulfilled a few more commitments in London, including the pleasant task of planning a tour to the Lakes with Mr and Mrs Gardiner.

On several counts it was a scheme with attractions beyond the beauty of the Lake District itself. Just such a tour had been offered to Elizabeth a year ago by this aunt and uncle, and the apparent disappointment of only being able to go as far as Derbyshire had led to another unexpected encounter between Elizabeth Bennet and Fitzwilliam Darcy, and thus to their marriage. An additional pleasure for Elizabeth, often painfully embarrassed by her relatives, was that her husband justly esteemed her uncle and aunt despite two highly detrimental facts: Mr Gardiner was her mother's brother, and he earned his living by trade.

While waiting for their guests, an unexpected caller sent up her card: Lady Catherine de Bourgh. At Elizabeth's wish she was instantly admitted, even though she had never fully retracted her abusive comments about the marriage. On this occasion she confined herself to announcing she had decided to overlook the past. Husband and wife both made proper enquiries about her daughter.

"Well enough, thank you, considering her frail health, unfortunately one of the burdens of the highly-bred. I overcome it by force of character, but Anne's delicacy bestows unusual refinement. I see you look particularly blooming, Mrs Darcy; you were lively enough in the days I entertained you at Rosings, but your new life must be an additional tonic. This unlikely result could never have been foreseen from your visit to the Collins!"

Both Darcys spoke together.

"I thank you madam, I am quite well."

"I hoped for just such an outcome, and was fortunate enough to achieve it some months later."

"My distinct recollection," (obviously not to be disputed) "is that reluctance to leave the compelling family ties of Rosings twice caused you to delay your departure. Both your cousin and I noted your low spirits, but it was the Colonel, not you, who had a partiality for Miss Eliza Bennet, until I reminded him not to display marked interest in a girl without fortune or family. Your only observation was, 'A lively mind.' Nothing of the lover in that."

"A lively and discriminating mind," corrected Darcy, turning a guarded look upon his wife who struggled with a mixture of disgust at Lady Catherine's abominable manners, and a curiosity to hear more. This now had to be satisfied with the following words.

"You were not near so eloquent as the Colonel. What has happened to you since then had nothing to do with Rosings."

Maintaining this view was clearly a necessity for the speaker, which meant that the forbearance required of a nephew conveniently agreed with Darcy's own determination not to discuss the cause of his distrait mood at Rosings. Silence allowed his aunt to continue without a pause.

"But no more of this, I told you the past was to be overlooked. Mrs Darcy, you must be wanting news of Mrs Collins."

Elizabeth was a willing listener, eager for fresh news of Charlotte's new-born daughter, but far from pleased by the opening sentences.

"I accompanied my congratulations to Mrs Collins with a warning that she must get sons, otherwise, if she survives Mr Collins, she will be turned out of Longbourn in her old age. Just as your mother, Mrs Darcy, will be evicted by the Collins if your father dies first – which I suspect is likely."

Receiving no reply to this inexcusable statement, Lady Catherine then offered such full details of Mrs Collins' lying-in, the daily increase in health of both mother and child and the only proper regime for the baby, that Elizabeth almost believed her husband's aunt had been in attendance, and was quite certain she supervised the monthly nurse.

Poor Charlotte! Having determined to marry the foolishly verbose Mr Collins in return for the security of marriage and a settled home, she was now condemned to live in close propinquity to his 'esteemed patroness'. Lady Catherine's rank in society and her own elevated view of herself, made any comparison with her curate seem unlikely, but in fact they resembled each other in being uncontrollably garrulous. Less ignorant than Mr Collins, she might speak with greater authority but unfortunately demonstrated an equal lack of propriety or judgment. It said much for Charlotte's forbearance – and foresight - that she seemed in a fair way to becoming as essential to Lady Catherine as she was to her husband.

When Lady Catherine was impertinent enough to enquire about their expectations, Darcy intervened.

"How much time can you spare us? We shortly expect friends with whom we are planning a tour to the Lakes; will you take some refreshment with us all?" Hoping to precipitate the departure of his noble aunt, he was about to mention Mr Gardiner's connection with Mrs Bennet, when she interrupted.

"I am in some haste. I was expecting to find Henrietta at home to receive me, while Augustus is visiting Brighton with the Regent. Despite my letter she was unaccountably absent, but I am confident she will be waiting for me now."

Even more anxious than Darcy to protect her relatives from Lady Catherine's incivility, Elizabeth stood up to make her farewells, but the Gardiners were announced at that moment. As Darcy chose to mention only their names in his initial introduction, his aunt, who rarely listened carefully, believed she knew them by repute - the Garlingworths of Gloucestershire - and immediately began offering advice about how to travel and what to see. She was in no way inhibited by never having visited the area, and Mr Gardiner, who had walked over those hills in his youth, soon recognised her ignorance but politely listened to inaccurate and inappropriate recommendations. To that extent the meeting went off well, even if the travellers' plans had not been usefully advanced by the time Lady Catherine finally made her farewells. At the last minute she turned to Darcy, offering, with much emphasis on the inconvenience involved, to present Georgiana and Elizabeth at Court next year even if her own daughter's health still precluded such exertion.

"You are very good, but Lady Otterburn has recently presented them at a private Drawing-Room. Elizabeth's sister, Mrs Bingley, was also there."

"Your wife's sister? I most certainly would not have undertaken it. The Countess amazes me by choosing to feel superior to those niceties of propriety to which I pay particular attention. In my view, the higher the birth the more careful should be the observance." The truce with Lady Catherine seemed at an end; Darcy preferred an icy silence, but wondered if his wife would endure this final insult. Fortunately Mrs Gardiner's quick wits made her fidget noisily with a pile of books and maps, reminding Lady Catherine of further advice she wished to give. Then, perfectly unaware of having given offence, she made her farewells with a promise to wait on the Darcys at Pemberley in the near future.

Elizabeth was sorry to have her anger briefly renewed, for prior to that last pronouncement of Lady Catherine she had savoured every excess, and had even hoped to share her amusement with her husband. But that might not have been possible, since a proud man could hardly rejoice to see his noble kinswoman not only obtuse, but vulgar, in comparison with people of greatly inferior birth.

For the remainder of their visit the Gardiners talked of anyone and anything except Lady Catherine, so successfully restoring everyone's spirits that after their departure, Darcy joined his wife at the piano. He never would sing when others were present, and only infrequently when they were alone, but this time he was a most willing partner. While she hunted for additional music he offered a briefly dismissive comment about his aunt, but Elizabeth laughingly recommended him to find a positive advantage in Lady Catherine's discourtesy.

"I seem often to be obliged to her for promoting my happiness. Her first interference was her most successful, but as a result of today's visit you have spent more time singing with me than ever before. You are too critical of your own performance; I love to hear our voices together, and am willing to deny others the pleasure of hearing us if that is your preference."

That was Darcy's unshakeable determination, but he acknowledged greatly enjoying their evening, particularly in contrast to his noble aunt's abrasive presence, thus causing his wife to suggest, "Perhaps we need an occasional abrasive element of our own, to prevent us being complacent? Even without Lady Catherine's intervention, we might sometimes manage a small quarrel, just to ensure that the happiness of our union does not cause me to sink into slavish acquiescence and you to become bored."

But her husband responded gravely.

"Inevitably there will be disagreements between us, Elizabeth, and as we must speak honestly to each other they might even lead to dissension. I say this advisedly because on such occasions I may sound overbearing, while your tone of voice - apart from the encounter that changed my life - while honest, manages to be conciliating."

"Dearest Darcy, how can you be thinking like this? It was just a teasing remark and now seems badly misplaced after an evening of particular pleasure."

"Indeed you are quite right. Why should I attempt to introduce a discord? When the need arises we shall learn how to deal with our problems, which are most likely to be caused by other people who need not concern us tonight."

Their occasional disagreements nearly always sprang from Darcy's formality opposed to Elizabeth's easier attitude, an inevitability considering their backgrounds, but usually susceptible to reasonable compromise.

Another question really pained Darcy, but he could hardly present it as a disagreement, it being impossible to explain his dislike of the increasing friendship between Mrs Cartwright and his wife. Within a week they would all leave London, but Darcy's efforts to avoid the Cartwrights would be frustrated for a few more days. They were all to be fellow guests at Broughton Castle, home for five centuries to the Fiennes, a family long raised to the Barony of Saye and Sele. Darcy had a particular affection for this place.

∾∾

Scene Five

∾∾

Darcy had developed this romantic affection for Broughton in his youth, but a blood connection between the Darcys and the Fiennes existed in France over six hundred years ago. This had been further consolidated when representatives from both families joined the entourage of their cousin, Eleanor of Castile, on her regal journey to marry the future King Edward I of England. The association was now very slender, in part because not every Darcy wished to remember that their ancestors had sprung from an illegitimate, junior branch of the Fiennes. Regardless of this, when Fitzwilliam Darcy went up to Oxford he was enough intrigued by the history of nearby Broughton to seek out his distant kinsman. As it happened, Lord Saye & Sele preferred his house in Kent, but they duly met in London and the Baron invited Darcy to visit Broughton whenever inclined - the steward and housekeeper would welcome some life about the place, most of which was becoming dilapidated, although there was comfortable lodging for a few people.

If Broughton had resembled Pemberley, young Darcy would not have felt the same degree of interest, but an almost deserted Tudor mansion, still containing substantial remnants of its medieval past, caught his imagination. An undergraduate at Oxford seeks for wider experiences than those available to a dutiful heir living with his parents on the family estate; consequently, the Baron and his son were destined to provide two of the major experiences of Darcy's immaturity. One was the romantic solitude of Broughton Castle, the other an introduction to the frivolous amorality of the Prince of Wales and his circle. Neither experience was regretted, but his present wish to share Broughton with his wife was equalled by a firm intention to avoid any closer connection with the Prince's Carlton House set. Very properly he had withheld specific names (including the Fiennes) when telling Elizabeth in general about his amorous past, and from now on saw no need for any further allusion to that aspect of his bachelor life. He was unaware that she had misapprehended him, following her own preferences in assuming that his involvement with women ended with the foolish days of early manhood he had described.

Darcy's thoughts were more prosaic as they approached the final mile of their journey, where the muddy lane below high banks, proved difficult to negotiate. He was surprised that his bon vivant cousin had chosen such an unsettled time of year to open up a long-deserted house; the rooms would be chilly, the beds damp. Fortunately, neither his wife nor his sister was likely to complain about minor discomforts; at this moment they were looking eagerly out of the coach commenting upon the hawthorn blossoms already over-blown in this sheltered spot.

They had already entered the park before the gatehouse brought them to the courtyard full of bustling activity, which continued indoors where there was a fire in the Great Hall, servants to escort them to their rooms, and their host awaiting them in the Parlour. But, as often happens, this visit to which Darcy had looked forward, now gave him little pleasure. The increased warmth and comfort merely emphasized the damp walls, mildewed hangings, and plaster ready to fall from ceilings; he wondered that his noble kinsman was not ashamed to be confronted by decades of neglect.

On the contrary, Lord Saye & Sele apologized light-heartedly for the shortcomings of his ancestral home compared with his other, less antiquated, country house. He knew that his guests (only four people in addition to the Darcys and the Cartwrights) all felt a concern for Broughton and therefore might appreciate an early opportunity to acquire *objets* of aesthetic or nostalgic appeal. Young Dominic Cartwright could offer detailed information, but this was by no means the main purpose of the party, for sooner or later there would be a major sale, as Belvedere, in Kent, was now the family's principal seat. Consequently, this was the last time he would entertain at Broughton and he greatly appreciated making his adieux in sympathetic company. It would be interesting to hear from Fitzwilliam Darcy what changes he noted since his last visit, in all probability almost a decade past.

Elizabeth, freed from a lingering fear that her host might be enduring a painful loss, was ready to enjoy everything. Unfortunately, her husband was noticeably out of spirits. To a certain degree she understood a feeling of dejection following unreasonably high expectations, but his sombre mood continued the following morning. Fellow guests, particularly the Cartwrights, were treated almost brusquely, and he was continually trying to lead her away from them with no other purpose, it seemed, than to deplore every sight that met his eyes. Hoping to soften his attitude she drew him to a window overlooking the garden.

"This place is utterly unlike Pemberley, but it entices me. It seems so solitary and hidden away, belonging to the fairytales we all loved in our youth, and consequently ideal material for any Gothic novel. I am surprised not to see ivy growing over the windows and cobwebs covering the furniture. When you came here alone, were you somewhat under the influence of those novels, or were you always too wise?"

"I have told you too much about my youth to be able to claim unusual wisdom. I was attracted to Broughton in just the ways you describe, but now those feelings have all passed and I am left deploring the neglect and waste."

"So shall we mark down things to save from strangers? Can wallpaper can be removed from walls? For our private sitting room I covet those lovely birds, trees and flowers covering the walls of more than one chamber. Mr Cartwright says they are hand-painted Chinese, which explains why I have never seen their like."

Darcy, feeling ashamed of his black mood, began to lead his wife out-of-doors, first stopping to look again at the Chinese wallpaper, before reminding her to wear heavier boots against the damp of the water meadows. He even suggested, after half an hour of exploration, that they walk towards the walled garden, from which they could hear voices. The years had made a wilderness out of a formal garden, and Darcy struggled to close a gate entangled with briars and a rusty lock, leaving his wife to walk ahead of him.

"Mrs Darcy I have been hoping for your company," said the familiar voice of Mrs Cartwright.

"And I for yours," said Elizabeth, remembering the invariable warmth of her welcome, compared with the careful distance maintained by younger women during the London Season.

Elizabeth had not the slightest suspicion that Mrs Cartwright had reasons to feel a greater antagonism than any of those young women. A predetermination to detest the new Mrs Darcy had been disarmed by the girl's unaffected, yet lively, manners, and suddenly the ex-mistress decided to make a friend of the wife and thereby embarrass the husband with a certain amount of provocative teasing.

Mrs Cartwright continued,

"But I thought I saw Mr Darcy; how has he vanished?"

"Probably still tangled in the briars he struggled with on my behalf, but as there is no Sleeping Princess to be rescued he may have turned aside."

Darcy approached as the women started to discuss which particular aspects of Broughton most appealed to them. He bowed silently, but when challenged for his opinion answered fully, and was almost relaxing under Mrs Cartwright's intelligent questions when she suddenly added a sentence that seemed oddly irrelevant to Elizabeth but which clearly meant something to her husband. It was mischievous rather than malicious, but he was renewing his decision to avoid Mrs Cartwright at the very moment they encountered her son and his sister talking together earnestly.

Dominic Cartwright's unprepossessing appearance had actually facilitated his friendship with Georgiana. Her infatuation with Wickham having taught her to be cautious about physical charm, Cartwright's spindly frame and sallow complexion were almost as much in his favour as his knowledgeable conversation. Darcy, quite unaware that they had met rather frequently, was surprised to hear Georgiana, with the ease of established friendship, ask the young man a question.

"Have you, after all, brought your flute with you?"

"It always travels with me for my own private enjoyment, but no piano or harp could survive the damp that prevails here and I am not foolhardy enough to perform alone."

"Oh, just think how plaintive music on the flute - some traditional laments or folk songs - would suit these surroundings."

"I remember noticing in London that a group of your songs were scored for two voices." He turned to include Elizabeth and Darcy, "For you and your sister I think you said? Now if you two ladies happened to have suitable music with you, could you possibly accept a wind instrument to accompany you instead of the piano?"

Elizabeth had no idea of his musical skill. If he could not hold the tune accurately the singers would have some difficulty, but she confidently believed that Georgiana, despite being equipped with music, would refuse. As Darcy shared this expectation, both were surprised by her merely looking at Elizabeth for consent before accepting with every sign of pleasure. Their footsteps had now brought them out of the garden, and Elizabeth agreed to Mrs Cartwright's suggestion of continuing on the paths close to the castle, while Darcy excused himself to go in search of his host and a longer walk.

"You must have no anxiety, Mrs Darcy," said the elder lady, "about my son as a flautist; he has real talent, and the instrument is well suited to his way of life, constantly travelling as he does."

Elizabeth offered a civil compliment about his artistic abilities, a subject on which his mother was very willing to enlarge.

"If it had not been for this war he was the ideal person to make the Grand Tour. True, he is still only twenty, and it will soon be reasonable for him to spend a year or more in Italy - in the Lowlands too, where there is a painter he is particularly anxious to examine. He is too young for marriage now, but his studies may create a delay of many years although his means are adequate for a reasonable establishment."

This provided much to think of, but Elizabeth avoided the subject of marriage, choosing instead to praise his growing reputation as an art expert.

"He has made good use of his time by visiting all the collections made by the English 'Milordi' up to 1789 before these miserable wars. Fortunately, his birth gave him the entry to aristocratic houses; initially he was a student anxious to learn from renowned family collections, now he is increasingly valued as an expert. The condition of this place and its treasures really grieves him, as I believe it does your husband. I am sure they would both benefit from talking together."

Elizabeth doubted it, but scarcely knew why. She could at least reassure Darcy that young Cartwright had no designs on Georgiana - if that in any way explained his coolness to both mother and son. From her observation of the two young people nothing more than friendship seemed to exist, but in any case how could there be any rational objection if something stronger happened to develop? By birth, breeding and fortune the Cartwrights were firmly established in society.

There was little physical resemblance between the two women pacing the shabby gravel paths, but anyone listening to their conversation might have fancied a family bond. Both had a natural enthusiasm enabling them to be more often happy than unhappy; both were quick and intelligent (though inevitably the advantage of years had made one of them better informed). In particular, they also shared a sense of the ridiculous, capable of providing many entertaining moments. On this occasion it amused Mrs Cartwright to discomfort Darcy while intending no harm to his wife. Elizabeth's less complex reaction was pleasure in the company of an older woman naturally formed to be something of an advisor as well as friend.

Had she suspected a recent connection between Darcy and her new friend, her mortification would have been intense. It is one thing to hear your prospective husband honestly admit his past with women of a type you could never care for, quite another to develop a friendship with a woman to whom no breath of scandal was attached, but who, in fact, had been the most recent object of his attentions. However, neither of the people involved meant to tell her, though Darcy sometimes wondered if lack of openness was not more damaging to their union than embarrassing disclosure. Even as a rejected lover he had remained entirely true to Elizabeth, his present difficulty existed because his nature had not allowed him to dissemble a little with Mrs Cartwright. It was to be hoped time and absence would ease the situation.

The music that evening was delightful; the weather the following morning, enchanting, and with the next stage of their journey, Dufton Hall, already occupying his mind, Darcy's last full day at Broughton became pleasurable, despite the fact that Dominic Cartwright threatened to escort the Chinese wallpaper to Pemberley when it had been detached and restored. While Georgiana and her maid drove to Oxford to join Mrs Annesley on the return journey to London, her brother and sister travelled in the opposite direction, to the Bingleys' estate.

In contrast to the hint of reserve in her husband that was worrying Elizabeth, it was refreshing to note the open manners of the other couple. Jane was certain of her pregnancy and Charles full of pride and delight. Rejoicing with them, Elizabeth found her unnamed anxieties dispersing; her marriage was as strong as the Bingleys, but Darcy's complex nature was likely to make it less uniformly calm, nor could she match her sister's equability.

If Jane could ever be selfish, this might well be the occasion. The child, the new home, everything was so wonderfully absorbing, and her sister was ready to be involved in every aspect. Their mother, of course, had been voluble on the subject of baby linen and baby nurses, followed by unhelpfully detailed reports of her own courageously endured sufferings in childbirth. Fortunately, everyone agreed that the delicate state of Mrs Bennet's nerves made it impossible for her to be present at the birth of her first grandchild.

"But you will let us be here Jane? I want to be with you, and think how useful Darcy will be to Charles."

"My dearest sister, yes, as long as *your* state of health permits."

"Perhaps it is time for me to become a sober matron, but it is not yet my active wish. The ideal would be if I come to you for this child, and perhaps you will be in a suitable state to attend my first lying-in. After that everything will be comfortably familiar, though I do hope it will not become an annual event."

Jane tried to urge acceptance of whatever providence ordained, but Elizabeth still felt four or five children would be quite enough.

The conversation then turned to their unmarried sisters, Jane saying, diffidently, "I wonder at our father's decision to keep Mary mainly at home while Kitty is to pay us lengthy visits? My mother has less in common with Mary than with any of her children."

"This could mark his determination to provide more guidance. Our mother encourages Kitty to think of nothing but flirtation and courtship, and Lydia and Wickham threaten to be frequent visitors at Longbourn. Kitty is malleable and Lydia incorrigible. *Her* confidence and determination would be admirable if put to better use."

Jane reluctantly agreed with these strictures, but then praised Mary for making out a respectable path for herself. She was, of course, too kind to describe her as the plain child in a family admired for good looks, and Elizabeth always felt a personal guilt about Mary's relative isolation among her sisters.

"Poor Mary, how unlucky to be the third girl when the two eldest are developing a close bond, and in due course the two youngest show a definite affinity. I, as the sister closest to her, should have done more; but really I might have succeeded better if Lydia had been next in age to me; Mary's lack of humour is a barrier I cannot overcome."

Jane gently reminded her that Georgiana apparently shared that trait, but refrained from adding Darcy's name, believing it best for a wife to look kindly on her husband's idiosyncrasies. Elizabeth defended her views.

"I know this sounds unjust, but somehow Georgiana's hesitancy suits gravity better than Mary's..." she bit her lip unable to find an inoffensive way of describing Mary's noisy parade of learning, before continuing, "But our family experience determines me to be particularly attentive to middle children - and not to spoil the youngest."

"Or the eldest son; whatever his position in the family?"

"Most definitely not spoil the eldest son (if there is a son at all) since everyone at Pemberley will do that."

"Here we are planning to avoid all the usual mistakes of parents; will we really manage to be wiser?"

Jane had meant this as a generality and was rather shocked that Elizabeth said firmly: "We must do better than our parents did."

It was necessary to change the conversation, so Jane concluded, "At dinner Charles will want to give you news of Caroline. There seems to be a growing attachment between her and a very suitable man, Mr Forbes, whose estate is about ninety miles south of London."

They exchanged a conscious look, but both decided against discussing if this was far enough from Dufton Hall. As Bingley would always make Jane's sisters welcome, she would not fail in the same courtesy, but she envied Elizabeth's genuine affection for Georgiana. Elizabeth, always uneasy about caring more for Darcy's sister than for Mary or Kitty, determined to compensate for these feelings by actively promoting their happiness. By nature they were not as calculating as Charlotte Collins - some real or imagined affection would be a prerequisite for marriage - but so far they had looked no higher than Meryton society and the recent welcome addition of young officers in the militia. The heightened expectations encouraged by their mother because their elder sisters had married so prosperously were unlikely to be fulfilled without overall improvement in their conversation and general demeanour. Sensible men of property would not be drawn to penniless girls of weak understanding and foolish behaviour.

These gloomy thoughts about members of her family were modified, following their return to Pemberley, by the arrival of Aunt Gardiner, whose conversation and bearing Mary and Kitty would have been well advised to emulate.

For Elizabeth, it was an additional gratification that her aunt and uncle also provided an admirable example of domestic felicity, and this after ten years of marriage. It was Darcy who had suggested the four children stay at Pemberley while the adults were touring the Lakes, and the invitation having been gratefully accepted, Mrs Gardiner brought her sons and daughters - with a governess and nursemaids - a week early to get everyone settled. Knowing that even well behaved children can be a strain for other people, their mother initially tried to keep them out of Darcy's way, but he actively sought their company.

"You must remember that from about the age of fourteen I had a small sister beseeching her brother to play with her. When our mother died I recognised an even stronger claim, even though my father was a devotedly tender parent. Enjoying the company of your children brings happy memories; it was easier to be a successful brother to a little girl than the guardian of a young lady making her debut in the world."

"Yet Georgiana is the most amiable, most talented, sister imaginable, and commendably mature for her age."

Elizabeth emphasised the last words, bearing in mind that Georgiana was developing preferences not shared by her brother. Another train of thought followed. Five months of mutual happiness still left her with some uncertainties about her husband's character; his excellent principles, his capacity to love, were undoubted, but although his pride was now under firmer control, in most circumstances he continued to dominate and others to submit.

In their marriage she knew her influence would always cause him to reconsider, but if they could not agree his decision would prevail. She could accept the general rule, however provoking on some occasions, for all husbands and fathers enjoyed this right however slender their moral claim. Her concern (based on his attitude to his sister) was that Darcy would be too inflexible a father. Georgiana usually deferred to him on all points, and should she venture to disagree was quickly silenced by her brother's disapproval. The habit of protection was so strong that he was reluctant to let her make friendships or form opinions running counter to his own. Expecting total compliance from a sister of marriageable age, would he not prove even more dictatorial to young children?

Watching him with these boys and girls provided a degree of reassurance. Surely he would become less adamant when Georgiana reasoned more firmly? Suddenly Elizabeth was confronted by her own unsound reasoning. How ridiculous that a daughter of the Bennet household should be advocating greater licence for girls. Having blamed her father for not controlling his younger daughters, she now found fault with Darcy because he did control his younger sister. Chastened, but quickly recovering, she promised herself the pleasure of congratulating him on having all the qualities to be as admirable a father as he was a husband - but preferably not in the near future.

ري

Scene Six

ري

The Lake District lived up to every expectation, including that of heavy rainfall. Some of the most famous vistas were shrouded in mist, but affectionate companionship, with the additional consolation of works by Gilpin and Wordsworth, compensated for these disappointments. Every reasonably dry moment was enjoyed to the full, with Mr Gardiner persuading the other three (instinctively loyal to the beauties of Derbyshire) to admit the superior claims of mountains and lakes, although Darcy could not resist noting that torrents of rain were apparently essential for the most dramatic effects. Of the four travellers his temperament was the least equable, but physical discomfort meant little to him; that he always commanded the best service available was due to his sense of consequence rather than any need for luxury. On this occasion his instinct to control the affairs of all around him fortunately suited the holiday inclinations of Mr Gardiner, who even deemed it an advantage that sudden changes of plan might result in some business letters remaining uncollected. Innkeepers were instructed to forward them to Pemberley.

By the time they had reached Lancashire on their homeward journey, fine days far outweighed wet ones in their shared recollections. Then the pleasures of domestic life began to make their claim, so when they turned in at the lodge gates of Pemberley, the Darcys rejoiced in the sight of home and the Gardiners' thoughts were full of their children. Unfortunately, their plans to stay for two days before moving on to the Bingleys had to be changed after reading letters forwarded from the Lake District. As urgent business awaited Mr Gardiner in Cheapside they must be on their way to Dufton Hall in the morning, leaving Mrs Gardiner and the children there while her husband continued by post-chaise to London. An express was immediately dispatched to Dufton, followed by all the activity involved in readying eight people for travel next day.

Two letters from Georgiana and one from Mrs Annesley had also been redirected, but as the writers themselves would arrive in the morning they were left unopened until the Gardiners' departure was organised. Elizabeth was half inclined not to open them at all to spare Georgiana the disappointment of repeating anecdotes only just read in the delayed letters, but of necessity they must be glanced through in case there was any alteration to travel plans. There was a change, which Mrs Annesley inappropriately considered an advantage. Mr Cartwright had offered to escort the ladies on the road to Pemberley by driving his own curricle while the Chinese wallpaper joined the servants and the luggage. Would it be agreeable to her brother and sister, asked Georgiana, for Mr Cartwright to be received at Pemberley? She was writing to the Inn at the mid-point of their journey to leave plenty of time for a reply. The last night of their journey from London would be spent at Kympton, and then she longed to be reunited with them at Pemberley, hearing all the details of their excursion. It was delightful to know she would have at least a few hours with the Gardiners and those dear little boys and girls.

Darcy reacted sharply.

"An entirely unsuitable idea; what could Mrs Annesley be thinking of? She knew our family party at Pemberley was to have two weeks alone; she herself goes to her married daughter for the summer. Our wishes were perfectly understood, yet without warning she foists this intruder on us. I am disappointed in her; a good deal of Georgiana's welfare depends on her discernment which now has to be called into question. Cartwright's presence is certainly not agreeable to me; what possessed Georgiana to think it might be?"

Elizabeth, finding herself in total disagreement, seized on one point.

"We were meant to receive these letters ten days ago, which would have given us time to answer. Naturally we do not want an extended visit, but he might reasonably stay for the same few days as Mrs Annesley. Presumably only a little time will be needed for supervising the wallpaper. We already enjoy the room for being so desirably private to ourselves, but we shall delight in it even more when it is furnished to our taste. Further decoration has been waiting upon the Chinese paper."

Her husband's ill temper made him correct her in a surprisingly unfriendly manner.

"I perceive it as particularly your room with everything, including this wallpaper, reflecting your choice. I leave it entirely to you, but merely add that I do not trust Cartwright or consider his chosen career suitable for a gentleman. An art expert is just about respectable, but a man who hangs wallpaper is not."

Elizabeth, offended by his denial that the room was to suit the tastes and needs of them both (their first joint endeavour since her arrival at Pemberley), decided to concentrate on Cartwright rather than display hurt feelings.

"Once he has established himself I imagine this type of enterprise will no longer be required of him. Indeed, this may be a personal favour either to Lord Saye & Sele, or to you."

"Certainly not to me."

"Well, to Georgiana." Even as she spoke Elizabeth felt how unwelcome this comment would be, but thinking it reasonable, continued quickly, "He has been invaluable to me as well. He is amazingly learned for such a young man, and generously shares this knowledge. We were able to visit two of the private collections which he is cataloguing and re-arranging at the moment, and also see the Turner watercolours on display in Mr Fawkes' London house."

"I was not aware of this."

"Possibly not." Elizabeth, feeling less conciliating, was in no mood to prepare Darcy for the 'Landscape with Ruins' she had chosen with long and happy deliberation under Cartwright's guidance. "There was nothing untoward about the arrangement. He is so frequent a visitor to Georgiana and Mrs Annesley at Eaton Square I am surprised you have never encountered him there. Being musical, in addition to his other talents, makes him an eminently suitable person for Georgiana to meet in the way of friendship. As for any stronger feelings: on her side I would think him too unprepossessing, and on his side, Mrs Cartwright told me he is only twenty, and will not marry until he has been able to spend a few years in Italy."

"Mrs Cartwright!" said Darcy contemptuously.

They were standing on an ornamental bridge where Darcy wished to show his wife the particular charms of the view in midsummer, but instead of enjoying the beauty and harmony they were both growing angry.

"Why do you dislike Mrs Cartwright? When we were introduced you did not warn me against her. Everyone speaks well of her, and it so happens I find her a particularly agreeable companion. This strong aversion seems unaccountable."

They had been leaning over the bridge and now turned towards each other; Darcy remained silent but the colour had risen in his face and in that moment Elizabeth instinctively understood the nature of the past relationship between her husband and Mrs Cartwright. A wish to conceal the feelings which threatened to overwhelm her, made her turn her head away. Her husband, almost relieved, took her hand, but whatever length of silence might have followed was broken by the unexpected sight and sound of a curricle approaching at a rapid pace; it would soon draw level with them before reaching the house. Was it a friend arriving unannounced - or urgent news from Kympton?

Darcy began to lead his wife forward, but she urged him to hurry ahead leaving her to follow. A moment's pause did not so much calm her spirits as turn her agitation into another channel, for the figure holding the reins was briefly close enough to be recognised as Dominic Cartwright. When Elizabeth reached the carriage entrance she joined her husband, who stood to one side intent on a letter, while Cartwright gave his weary horses into the charge of his manservant.

"All is well with Georgiana and Mrs Annesley, but the Kympton family is in great trouble. A highly infectious strain of putrid fever has developed in the village, and both Mrs Gervase and the baby have been stricken. The young sister is doing her best, but they cannot find any satisfactory help locally, so Gervase appeals to us - for his parishioners as well as for himself - knowing Lambton has several experienced nurses. You must consult with Mrs Reynolds, Elizabeth; we will hope to send nurses and useful supplies by coach tomorrow, but I shall leave today to talk with Gervase.

"After you have greeted Cartwright and arranged with Mrs Reynolds, you and I must discuss another way in which we can assist the Gervase family. It is a minor contribution, but will affect our daily life in the next weeks."

He gazed at her intently, before handing her the letter and arranging to meet after her interview with Mrs Reynolds. That excellent woman, adding useful suggestions of her own, arranged everything, leaving Elizabeth free to continue Georgiana's letter.

Old Mrs Gervase and the elder Miss Porter had travelled with Georgiana, having been her guests in London before the departure. Even amid the pressing anxieties, Elizabeth thought how Darcy would deplore an increasing intimacy with the Porters. The explanation, however, was simple. As sea air had been recommended for Mrs Gervase' health, she, with Maria Porter in attendance, had visited Hove, staying with Georgiana on the way south, and most gratefully accepting the chance of being taken all the way home on the return journey. A message explaining the anxious situation had missed them in Hove, but yesterday Mr Gervase met them at the parsonage gates, requiring them to use the Inn at the next village until other arrangements could be made. It was obvious what those arrangements must be, and Darcy joined her within minutes to agree that the two ladies must come to Pemberley.

Then he was ready to depart, hoping to arrive at Kympton before dark and, assuming there was nothing more to be done for Gervase, escort Georgiana and her party to Pemberley the following day. Speaking only of the Kympton family they parted with scarcely an embrace, which might have been due to general

preoccupation and haste, but Darcy thought his wife
turned away too abruptly.

As soon as she was alone Elizabeth gave way to tears of
humiliation and resentment, hating Mrs Cartwright and
trying to keep her imagination from thoughts of her
husband with that woman. She wept over the deception
practised on her; the two of them sharing a secret, which
judging by Darcy's strained manners, she suspected
must belong to the fairly recent past and have been
painfully concluded. She unjustly included him in the
bitter feelings evoked by remembering the pleasure of
Mrs Cartwright's overtures of friendship, until
conceding that Darcy had, in fact, spoken as openly of
his past as the laws of gentlemanly behaviour permitted.
Even this acknowledgement could not overcome the
jealousy that attacked her.

Wearied by tears and an accompanying headache, she
had to face the solicitude of her maid. Was Mrs Darcy
well enough to dine with her guest? Cartwright! The
irony of the situation gave Elizabeth enough energy to
meet him at dinner. Earlier, when he had suggested
travelling to Kympton with his host, such a
disinclination for his company was manifested that
young Cartwright willingly accepted the sensible
arrangement of an evening with that delightful Mrs
Darcy instead. Fortunately for his expectations,
Elizabeth's sense of justice helped her appear much as
usual; a task made easier as only the briefest enquiries
about his mother were needed before the anxious
situation at Kympton dominated the conversation until
they retired for the night.

Tomorrow she would be meeting the mother-in-
law and sister of poor Mrs Gervase. What must they be
feeling, full of fears, wanting to help, yet powerless to

do so? She vowed (without success as far as that night was concerned) to put her own feelings aside, or at least direct her outrage solely towards Mrs Cartwright. But she almost wished her husband would be needed at Kympton; in daytime the attention due to old Mrs Gervase and young Miss Porter might effectively distract them, but at night there would be misery and awkwardness, with thoughts of that woman ever present. Even at that moment, anger and mortification were renewed by the conviction that when Darcy had spoken of past amours he in no way described Mrs Cartwright. Perhaps she had been the exception, and therefore exceptionally dear?

Unfortunately the difficulties fulfilled her worst expectations. Any further discussion seemed intolerable, but she must know what period of time had been involved.

The question was almost a relief to Darcy, who was already struggling for words to explain that the affair had ended for him when he re-encountered Elizabeth at Rosings. Not even the anguish of so unexpectedly having his love rejected had required any change in the wording of the letter prepared for Mrs Cartwright as soon as he decided to make Elizabeth Bennet his wife. The task had not been easy, for the writer was buoyed by ardent hopes while completely failing to understand the degree of suffering he was inflicting. He described his lasting admiration for Mrs Cartwright - then ended the relationship in words that allowed for no discussion.

Recalling the blundering insensitivity of these past actions was painful for Darcy, but his blameless wife suffered even more from hearing only a partial description of them. Elizabeth glanced briefly at her husband before looking away, not yet able to comprehend information that he hoped might moderate her pain. Then Darcy enquired, formally, if she preferred to have her bedchamber to herself, but Elizabeth, dreading such a specific break with conjugal habit, mutely shook her head. Rationally they both understood that this estrangement would pass, but while the husband's emotions more or less kept pace with his thoughts, his wife conducted a daily battle trying to make her feelings agree with her mental arguments.

Marriage having brought a new intensity to her love, she had not yet found consolation in the fact that his relationship with Mrs Cartwright developed at a time when not only did she herself heartily dislike him, but he was trying to deny his increasing interest in her. Resentment towards her husband was not the cause of their estrangement so much as Elizabeth's pain at knowing it was created by the one person who appeared to possess all the attributes she most admired.

At the very moment at Rosings when she, Elizabeth, was refusing Darcy's proposal of marriage, that woman was confidently awaiting his return to London. It was true he then broke with her, but she was now tormented by the thought that Mrs Cartwright's elegance of mind and person must linger in his memory.

It was not that Elizabeth lacked confidence in her own powers, including the blessing of an attractive appearance. However, in her estimation this last attribute never ranked highly; after all, she was a prime supporter of Meryton's view that Jane Bennet was the family beauty. She personally took greater pride in possessing an observant eye and a quick mind - qualities that fostered a reliance on her own judgement. The natural confidence thus engendered had easily sustained her in the unchallenging surroundings of Meryton and, despite some painful blunders in the recent past, continued to

sustain her after her arrival in London as the bride of
Fitzwilliam Darcy.

Now once again Elizabeth must condemn
herself for poor judgement. Her present sufferings were
intensified by the need to correct an unthinking
assumption that her husband's amorous life was
confined to the time before she first met him. Strive as
she would she could not keep her imagination in check,
and to these pangs were added the additional pain of
finding her estimate of Mrs Cartwright's visible
attractions had not altered. Had she been thinking
rationally such a fact would have caused no surprise, and
further rational thought might even have brought a less
adamant dislike for the defeated 'rival' who had been so
abruptly dismissed.

Darcy's emotions were solely concerned with his wife.
Their estrangement was grievous, but he understood
Elizabeth's unhappiness, and might not have felt entirely
content had she reacted with calm indifference. However
it was just as well the private sitting room was unfit for
use, because they lost all the intimacy and unreserve it
had been designed to promote. In the weeks before their
trip to the Lakes, this hitherto neglected room, furnished
to his mother's formal tastes, was already becoming as
dear to him as their bedchamber. There was always so
much he wanted to say to his wife. Not only was Darcy
proud to be her mentor, but for the first time in his life
he shed his instinctive reserve, offering her recollections
and private thoughts he had never shared with anyone
else. Now all this ease had vanished, although, by every
means available (short of an outright apology) he tacitly
disowned the unwarranted remark about the room being
solely for her pleasure.

The tension between man and wife alarmed
Georgiana and was subconsciously felt by the strangers

in the house. While being meticulously courteous, their host's manners were forbidding; he actively disliked Cartwright, was somewhat displeased with Mrs Annesley and regretted the increasing intimacy between Georgiana and Miss Maria Porter.

His first instinct was to avoid everyone by spending the greater part of his time in the Estate Office where forestry decisions were needed, until one day he offered Elizabeth a tentative invitation to join him there. She had a general idea of the Estate Yard occupying a great area behind the domestic offices, but her contact had primarily been with the carpenters and decorators working on the house - a minute part of the whole. Now Darcy took his wife into all the workshops to see the scores of men responsible for maintaining, not only the mansion itself, but the great woods, the roads, bridges, footpaths and fences, the ponds, lakes and streams throughout the Pemberley estate. Occupied together in this way they were almost content, particularly as these activities woke a warmer response in Elizabeth than Mrs Reynold's domain of domestic servants, store cupboards, linen presses and laundries.

The daily news from Kympton, which at first was all uncertainty, became increasingly optimistic. At Pemberley, Cartwright not only supervised the Chinese wallpaper, but also walked through the Long Gallery with Elizabeth and Georgiana making invaluable suggestions about adding to the pictures. Although the reasons eluded her, Georgiana accepted the fact that while her brother would not listen to any of that young man's ideas about Pemberley, he was prepared to benefit from them indirectly by attending to suggestions from his wife and sister.

As the hopeful messages continued from Kympton and Cartwright's visit ended, much of the strain was relaxed, and after a few more days even better news reached them. Recovery for both mother and child now seemed certain, and Bella Porter, despite spending day and night in the sick room, showed no sign of infection. Most heartily did the three Darcys share the relief felt by their guests, and that evening for the first time, they met in a mood of almost normal social intercourse.

Mrs Gervase had daily confided her sufferings to her hosts, expressing her gratitude for their hospitality with manners implying a shared intimacy. Maria Porter's reserve had conveyed even stronger anguish to Georgiana, who wondered that Mrs Gervase' tender feelings did not extend to her young relative, Maria. Of course they were not related by blood; the elder lady, on behalf of her son, might consider his wife's sisters an unreasonable burden. When she confided this to her brother Darcy, he observed:

"As Gervase seems able to offer affection as well as protection, his mother should follow his example. The girls appear to be entirely deserving, the lack of good breeding probably not being as noticeable at Kympton where they are useful members of the household. During this anxious time the elder sister has obviously been invaluable."

"The younger sister, Fitzwilliam. The Miss Porter who is with us is the elder, and deeply unhappy at not being at home. They are closely attached, having been parentless for five years, and Bella - the youngest - is only sixteen, almost the same age as myself. I doubt that in her situation I could have been equally useful and unselfish. Poor Maria says very little, but you can imagine how she longs to be of greater use."

Georgiana's words appealed to her brother's strong family affections even as he silently resisted any comparison between the lives of those young women and his sister, but he only commented: "She is performing a useful duty by being with Mrs Gervase. It was a decision made by her brother-in-law."

In spite of these dismissive words he determined to pay closer attention to the girl, though Mrs Gervase temporarily frustrated his intention. Relief had put her in a festive mood and she rambled inconsequentially about her own ancestors and the heirloom lace she was wearing. Her hosts began to find her tiresomely self-important, something they had not observed when Kympton had dominated the conversation. However, Darcy, not easily deterred from a chosen course, moved away to where Miss Porter sat. From her childish appearance and usual habit of reserve he expected to find her alarmed by his attention, so to start the conversation he gently reminded her that the messenger to Kympton would be leaving at an earlier hour tomorrow. She enquired eagerly if some goods were being transported that day.

"Miss Porter, whatever you want to send will of course be delivered for you."

"But will it be a man on horseback, or some wheeled transport?"

"The latter," said Darcy quickly changing plans, "if you can have your packages ready for seven o'clock."

"Not packages, Mr Darcy; I (as you may imagine) dearly want to see my family. If, without troubling anybody, space on the wagon could be found for me, I could spend an hour with Mr Gervase and Bella - out of doors if that is still required. And possibly even see my elder sister and the baby through a window. If such a thing... "

"My dear Miss Porter," interrupted Darcy, "you may not travel in a wagon! We can provide a suitable conveyance but your family must arrange somewhere for you to rest before the return journey. Gervase must be consulted."

A silence had fallen over the room allowing the other ladies to hear that last sentence, followed by Miss Porter composedly urging that there were friends who would almost certainly offer her rest and refreshment if that was the chief obstacle. Mrs Gervase' voice was suddenly raised.

"Maria, I am ashamed of you, inconveniencing Mr Darcy who has already done so much for you. How thoughtless and selfish; I really must apologise on your behalf."

"My enquiries Ma'am were to ensure I did not inconvenience Mr Darcy."

Maria Porter's quiet tones managed to be heard before Darcy added his assurance. Even while conceding Mrs Gervase' certain rights of authority he was affronted by the manner in which she interfered, and instantly began to think of solutions. But Mrs Gervase persisted in ill-advised arguments that disgusted all her unwilling listeners.

"You are too ready to neglect my needs; just because Mrs Darcy kindly provided me with a maid does not mean you are free of duties. You forget what you owe to my son."

"I shall never forget my love as well as my duty, but I think Mr Gervase would approve my wish to see his dear wife, and my younger sister who has undertaken all the anxious duties I longed to share."

Their host, at his most magisterial, announced that tomorrow's messenger would take a letter advising Gervase of Miss Porter's request, and given his approval suitable arrangements would be made as swiftly as possible. If Miss Porter were to stay a night or two with friends nearby, Mrs Gervase could be assured of every attention at Pemberley; perhaps it would be agreeable to her to withdraw to her apartments even now where Mrs Reynolds would be happy to discuss additional ways of enhancing her comfort? The disconcerted Mrs Gervase, wishing to retire with as much dignity as possible, tried to summon Maria with her eyes, but Darcy ceremoniously led her from the room, enduring her voluble thanks in silence. The three women who remained were equally silent until Maria Porter tactfully said good night; Darcy therefore returned to find his wife and sister alone, and with a greatly exaggerated gesture offered an arm to each of them saying, "Tonight I mean to assert control over the women under my roof. I seem to have lost the opportunity to banish Miss Porter to her room, so I shall have to be satisfied with domineering over a blameless wife and sister."

Georgiana's smile was a little uncertain, but Elizabeth was delighted. Her husband was not much given to pleasantries and in recent weeks she herself had been wearisomely grave and awkward. It was time for humour to re-enter their lives, and if Mrs Gervase were not found ridiculous she would soon become a great annoyance.

Within a few days Maria Porter made her visit to Kympton, and within two weeks she and the elder lady returned home. Uncomfortably aware that the return of a petulant old woman might be a tiring experience for the convalescent, the Darcys were not unselfish enough to urge her to extend her visit with them. Miss Porter, however, had grown daily in Darcy's estimation, not only her calm demeanour in the face of Mrs Gervase' incivility, but also her thoughtful replies when he engaged her in conversation. With no advantage of appearance or address, yet her confidence was greater than Georgiana's, due to a healthy mixture of intelligence, commonsense and self-respect. Admiring these qualities, Darcy himself expressed a general willingness to see. Maria Porter at Pemberley again, but even as his young sister thanked him she dared to make an alternative suggestion.

"Dear brother, we have all admired Bella Porter for her devoted nursing regardless of the cost to her own health. As soon as the family has enjoyed the pleasures of reunion would it not be a good idea to invite *her* to Pemberley, where she could enjoy a complete change from those heavy duties? As I am equally attached to both sisters, I would enjoy having Bella here – if it would not displease *you?*"

It would displease Darcy on several counts, but having already shown a degree of hostility to Georgiana's friend, young Cartwright, his brotherly affection led him to provide only one reason.

"A moment's thought will convince you such a plan would not be feasible in the immediate future, my dear. Unfortunately for us all, within a week our mother's old friend, Judge Jones, makes his annual visit to Pemberley before attending the Assizes. As you know to your cost, this has been a fixed date almost since your birth, Georgiana, and he must always be made welcome though I frequently disapprove of the sentences he hands down. When our local magistrates consult me about poachers caught on our land, I do recommend leniency wherever possible, for some are men desperate to feed hungry families, rather than being hardened criminals. Judge Jones does not discriminate, which makes him increasingly insufferable."

Looking at Elizabeth, he added, "I fear that, despite being forewarned, you will find his company hard to bear, my dear."

"Well, Darcy, as in the future we are likely to be more at Pemberley than you were in your wild bachelor days..." her husband smiled, her sister looked shocked, before Elizabeth continued. "Perhaps you are considering becoming a magistrate to counteract these tendencies?"

"Quite possibly, but not until you and I have time to consider the obligations involved. For now, I must ask Georgiana to postpone Bella Porter's visit until the Judge leaves."

Obviously his sister was in total agreement, but Elizabeth, approving the courage shown by making this request, offered another suggestion.

"But it will be highly appropriate a week or so later when our guests will be far better suited to the interests of a sixteen year old. My family are coming here, en route for the Bingleys, with the particular intention of having Mr Vere teach them all the latest dance steps, Bella would be sure to enjoy that – and Georgiana, who might otherwise have found it wearisome since she needs no instruction, will enjoy it on behalf of her friend."

Some details about this already familiar plan were tactfully omitted. London's most famous Dancing Master would be on hand to teach Mary and Kitty not only the newest dances, but also to advise about etiquette and deportment. Elizabeth's optimistic spirit dared to hope her mother might also benefit from observing Mr Vere's instruction in some of the social niceties that still eluded her. All this was in preparation for a week of festivities at Dufton Hall where the gregarious Charles Bingley had arranged a reunion of friends from college days - several of them still unmarried.

Darcy instantly grasped the advantages of providing Georgiana with her own friend on this occasion. He knew that Elizabeth was always uneasy when the Bennet girls and his sister were thrown together for any length of time as the young ladies created an ill-assorted trio. On behalf of his wife and sister, Darcy therefore immediately elevated Bella Porter's need for a week of youthful pleasures to a priority. Furthermore, ensuring that their guests enjoyed themselves might help the Master and Mistress of Pemberley overcome their remaining difficulties.

When the Bennet family arrived, mother and daughters unanimously approved the alarming Miss Darcy being mainly occupied with her friend. They already knew of the crisis endured by the Gervase family, and meeting Miss Bella Porter increased their general feelings of benevolence. She looked scarcely grown-up, her person was unremarkable and her clothes pathetically plain. Being a cheerfully talkative girl, Darcy considered her a less impressive character than her sister, although his wife reminded him that she was a sixteen-year-old just released from weeks of responsible and exhausting duties.

There were different excursions every day, riding lessons for the uninitiated, and hours of dancing in the evening, enjoyable despite the absence of male partners. It was never expected that Mr Bennet would dance, and Darcy was scarcely more obliging since he joined them only once - in order to waltz several lengths of the Long Gallery with his wife while Mr Warriner, dashingly unclerical in movement, was happy to partner Georgiana. Despite his good intentions, Darcy continued to find Mrs Bennet almost unendurable and his 'sisters', Mary and Kitty, under-bred and under-educated. It must be admitted he suffered little from their conversation as in his presence both were terrified into silence.

Then suddenly the number of available men was increased with the arrival of Colonel Fitzwilliam, en-route for his family home at Otterburn. Elizabeth, fearing her mother's blatant attempts to gain husbands for her daughters, earnestly advised her that the Colonel had no fortune and was generally believed to need a wife to supply this deficiency.

She need not have worried. He was courteous to everyone, unfailingly attentive to Georgiana and herself, but otherwise depressed both in health and spirits. For a moment Darcy wondered (having observed his behaviour at Rosings) if Elizabeth was the cause, but when the two cousins were alone, the Colonel disclosed the sorry condition of his regiment - suffering as much from disease as from enemy attacks - and the purpose of this brief visit to England. Awaiting him in Otterburn were private supplies to improve the situation; excellent organisation and further funds were available. Darcy's offer of a generous contribution was gladly accepted.

Mrs Bennet knowing nothing of this, presented her views.

"Well Kitty, there is not much chance for you there, as it seems likely the Colonel has always been destined for that unfriendly Miss Darcy. Good luck to them both for he is not much more entertaining than she is - although Lizzy cried him up amazingly as if he could be compared with Bingley or Wickham.

"Nor is there much to be hoped from that Mr Warriner, whose stipend at Pemberley is a miserable two hundred pounds - and no glebe land to farm. Admittedly there is almost no work to be done, but most parsons are idle, and no doubt Darcy could easily increase it or find him another living."

Kitty conceded, "Warriner's dancing did surprise me, and I wouldn't have minded a turn at the waltz with him instead of being partnered by a stupid sister (though I must say it wasn't so bad when Lizzy replaced Mary). But I certainly hope to do better than a man who babbles on about flowers and never seems to notice anything about the person he is talking to."

She was rebuked.

"You are not the only daughter in this family who needs a husband, and much as I dislike all this going about in society, unfortunately all the work is left to me, your father being too disobliging to involve himself in these matters. It was not you, but Mary, in my mind as a possible Mrs Warriner, as apparently the man is reckoned quite a scholar despite appearing such a simpleton. I am told that is sometimes the way, though no-one could accuse your father of not being sharp enough in conversation."

"If she likes him, good luck to her. He is certainly an improvement on..." began Kitty, before hastily recollecting the danger of any reference to Mr Collins and therefore substituting 'most clergymen'.

Fortunately her mother had been musing over the following ideas.

"Now if Mary happened to take his fancy they would have few household expenses, for Lizzy could see to all their provisioning. But on second thoughts you know, she had better not take him even if he offers for I look to the Darcys to supply better suitors than Warriner."

While Kitty (despite previous experience of the speed with which her mother envisioned potential husbands for her daughters) marvelled at this example of a man being dismissed before he had demonstrated even a modicum of interest, Mrs Bennet continued.

"Just fancy, Darcy refuses all contact with Wickham, so Mr Bennet gets the begging letters instead, and obstinately refuses to pass them on to Lizzy who could easily contrive something. It all has a terrible effect on my poor nerves, though I still have a soft spot for Wickham, scamp though he is. Jane will just have to get something from Bingley.

"If only Lizzy were a more biddable daughter I could teach her how to coax money from her husband, who fortunately dotes on her despite his stiffness to everyone else. Though for my taste there has always been something irritating about Lizzy's manner - too many of her father's odd ways which are not very becoming in a girl. However, I admit she puts some life into Darcy and his sister. She has married better than I ever hoped, and now must help me find husbands for you and Mary."

Mr Bennet moved on to Dufton once the frivolities of the house party were over, but Bella Porter continued her visit, bringing the same cheerful spirit to a different set of activities. She accompanied Georgiana to the Sunday Schools, which had fallen to the care of Farmer Biggs' sister, newly returned from her Seminary.

This young lady had been taken aback to find herself apparently in charge soon after expressing a casual interest to dear Mr Warriner, and even more surprised that her initial conversation with him was almost the last. He became amazingly elusive, and when hunted down repeated his thanks and protested his own total incompetence. Poor Miss Biggs, greatly relieved to find that Miss Porter was trained as a governess, invited the young ladies to continue discussing the Schools, at her home, Pleasant Valley Farm. There Georgiana listened admiringly while the other two planned practical projects and discarded the impossible hope of providing daily education to a few of the brightest children. It was more than Miss Biggs could undertake.

Darcy observed this new connection with mixed feelings. The Biggs family, in general demeanour fitting the description of minor gentry, in sober fact ranked as tenant farmers, while Bella Porter, whose aspirations should realistically remain at the same level, was now known as Miss Darcy's friend. The Porter sisters had won his respect, and their homely manners were noticeably improved, but obviously their chances of finding husbands among the visitors to Pemberley were slender. Miss Biggs might well be more use to them, but all kinds of difficulties would arise with any continued interaction between the two social groups. Georgiana's attachment to the girls was warmer than his, but his mind was better equipped to see where their best advantage lay.

Elizabeth was pleased that Georgiana had found appropriate help, for her own interests were much more inclined to the Estate Yard. It had the additional advantage of allowing her to learn from her husband, a situation that suited them both. This shared activity, joined to the passage of time, had almost dismissed Mrs Cartwright from her mind, but undoubtedly the final cure for her jealousy was the knowledge that she was expecting her first child. If this was a little earlier than they originally hoped, both of them now felt the pregnancy aptly marked a renewal of happiness and agreed that spring was the perfect time of year for a baby to be born.

They had already planned to be mainly at Pemberley for the remainder of the year, entertaining their friends rather than being entertained, but Darcy became anxiously protective, urging immediate changes in daily life. There must be no more taking the reins of the phaeton when driving around the park, and most particularly, no more riding until the baby was safely born. Having gone to no little trouble to discourage Elizabeth's old habit of walking, he now urged it as the safest, healthiest, form of exercise and one he would be happy to share; they could walk or drive to specific areas they had been studying together on the estate maps. If she ever walked out alone beyond the immediate parkland and gardens visible from the house (which he hoped would be a rare occasion) not only must one of the dogs accompany her, but she must announce the route and keep to maintained paths.

As Elizabeth had not intended pregnancy to make great changes in her daily life, the numerous restrictions were rather daunting. Knowing that Darcy's mother's history had implanted these fears she waited patiently for him to see that her own constitution was entirely different, and ultimately her robust health calmed most of his anxieties. They were, as promised, at Dufton for the birth of Jane's son towards the end of the year and even spent some time in London before returning home for the last months.

ৎ৶৯

Scene Seven

ৎ৶৯

In Derbyshire, the late arriving spring was welcomed with particular joy; sentiments also applying to the Darcys' daughter, Cecilia, whose healthy birth was delayed by three weeks. Elizabeth grew thoroughly weary of waiting, but was able to joke that the baby knew her Aunt Jane should be present, and therefore refused to appear until young Charles Edward Bingley (four months her senior) recovered from an indisposition. During this period her husband's sufferings might be judged more painful than her own, haunted as he was by the miscarriages and infant deaths blighting his parents' marriage. Anything unexpected and untoward was almost insupportable for Darcy and it required the uncomplicated delivery of a healthy infant to quiet the worst of his fears.

The Bingleys were still at Pemberley, Jane's calm confidence being of great assistance to Elizabeth who was not innately maternal. About her own health she was much more decisive and even before the formal month's lying-in was over, demanded to spend almost as much time downstairs as upstairs, to her husband's mixed pleasure and anxiety. That date now well passed, she was on her way one morning to Georgiana's sitting room, but catching sight of Darcy started down the staircase, which he mounted at great speed.

"Elizabeth you promised me not to do this alone."

"Nor would I have done so, for my intention was to join Georgiana and Jane, but the prospect of your company is even more attractive. I assumed you and Charles would be out of doors in such lovely weather, but now I can ask you to drive me round the park; Cecilia is just this moment asleep, the sun is shining, and think how safe and happy I shall be with you driving the phaeton – through the beech avenue, please, for the newly opened leaves must be that perfect shade of tender green. There are beautiful vistas from our windows, but I want to be out of doors with you."

The way the request was phrased held great charm for a man who sorely missed the daily companionship of his wife, but these charms were not powerful enough to persuade him to any risky action. He paused to consider the dangers of her being chilled by the wind or jolted by the movement of the carriage, for he found it impossible to take Elizabeth's excellent health for granted. A moment's thought determined him that his own presence – in addition to extra wraps and cushions – would be safeguard enough.

After a period of sullen skies and a cold wind, on this morning only a few clouds dappled the blue sky, allowing the sun to shine on an English landscape, beautiful at any season but briefly a miracle of freshness as spring advanced. Darcy planned to show his wife not only the beeches but also a cluster of rare wild flowers, invisible last year but blooming now.

Elizabeth, in high spirits at the prospect of an outing, hoped to tease him from the role of over-anxious husband by recalling the time before they were married.

"Now I recollect that the little dell where you are to show me the fritillaries was the first place in which we were alone together at Pemberley. Somehow this small detail has not previously occurred to either of us."

Darcy was energetic in his response.

"It may not have occurred to you, dearest Elizabeth, but that very moment has a strong claim on my memory."

"You have taken me completely by surprise. What I recall is an awkward, rather than a romantic, moment when we left my aunt and uncle on the level path and walked down to the ornamental grotto. I could not overcome my embarrassment at being at Pemberley uninvited, and your welcoming manner, being so totally unexpected, only increased my awkwardness. How slow I was to realize we were both assailed by a growing affection we had no ability to communicate. And now," Elizabeth continued with a smile, "impossible as it seemed then, here we are comfortably together, all mysteries unravelled, the appropriately sober and sedate parents of a child."

As everything in her manner denied these adjectives, her husband responded on his own behalf.

"My looks belie me if sobriety implies a lack of strong feelings, but I am thankful to be spared the ferment I endured on that occasion. *I* can recall every detail. You held your hands under the water."

"Did I?" said his wife doubtfully. "Yes, I believe I did. Returning to the scene will revive my memory."

They walked to where a modest flow fell close to the footpath, and Elizabeth, removing her gloves and stretching her hands to the water, exclaimed happily, "Now I am reminded of the surprising coldness of that little waterfall. It was a distraction, an activity to cover a difficult silence; I wonder why your recollection is so much sharper than mine?"

"Because, until that moment, it so happened I never had the chance to touch your ungloved hand - the only part of a woman a male acquaintance might with any propriety touch – and... "

"I remember, I remember," cried Elizabeth triumphantly, but allowing him to continue.

"I used my handkerchief to dry your hands – just as I do now. It was over in a minute, otherwise I would have been forced to relinquish the task to you, but it was etched into my memory as perhaps the closest physical contact I might ever be permitted. Two years ago I was in agony, fearing you might never love me. Yes, what a magnitude of changes time has brought, but (I see from your eyes, your smile, you know my feelings, beloved woman) my passion for you has in no way been transformed into the calmness of settled habit.

"What has changed is that our marriage has been blessed with a child. Now it becomes my duty to watch over you both until the baby's health is established and yours re-established. If such a thing is possible, it is a serious but joyful task."

Reassuringly, he now looked more joyful than serious, for although solicitously attentive while his wife climbed up the slope and into the carriage, she moved so confidently and looked so blooming, his fears were almost laid aside.

Elizabeth's thoughts had lingered in the past, struck by the intensity of his recollections. How incomplete had been her understanding of his feelings that day; her own emotions, confused as they were by a decided aversion giving way to increased respect, were calm by comparison with Darcy having to conceal the strength of his passion over many months of uncertainty. She gazed at him tenderly, indebted to him for loving her even when his love seemed hopeless.

Absorbed in the pleasure of each other's company, they forgot the wild flowers until a cluster of them appeared at their feet.

When they returned - having stayed longer than Darcy originally intended - they found the Bingleys reading their letters; one from Mrs Bennet was addressed to both Jane and Elizabeth.

Their mother confirmed that all the family would arrive at Pemberley within a few days to see the baby before she and the girls returned with the Bingleys to Dufton Hall. Then she rambled on.

"And how I long to see that dear little Charles Edward – not before time - as you have done nothing of that sort since your son was born. And how I long to see that dear little Charles Edward again. Jane, our visit to you will be just the moment to start putting your sisters in the way of suitable men. Dufton's splendidly redecorated reception rooms should be celebrated by a Ball. Thank heavens for a boy in the family at last, and so fine and strong. Lizzy must hope for better luck next time, Darcy will be expecting an heir - though at least there is no wicked entail to ruin the family after his death."

The sisters read quickly through the familiar diatribe about 'those grasping Collins', finally reaching a note in their father's hand. He would remain at Pemberley with the Darcys, thus avoiding the company of prospective suitors until he was assured of suitable offers; preferably one apiece for Mary and Kitty, with fortunes about equal to avoid any dissension. He could come down to Dufton at a day's notice.

There were other letters, including one from Charlotte Collins repeating her affectionate congratulations along with helpful advice should Cecilia develop red gum; it was important to recognise the first signs. She hoped there might soon be an opportunity for them to meet; their infant daughters added a new dimension to a longstanding friendship.

This was typical of Charlotte's genuine affection, but Elizabeth also identified an ulterior purpose - the hope that Darcy's patronage in the Church would assist Mr Collins at some future date. Charlotte, who bore the undiluted burden of his company, possibly deluded herself that her friends could tolerate an occasional dose of that ignorant verbosity, but Elizabeth (for her own sake as much as her husband's) could not bear to entertain Mr Collins, and a reunion centred on Longbourn and Lucas Lodge was even less feasible. At Pemberley he would disgust Darcy even as he tried to ingratiate himself, and at Longbourn he would adopt some uncomfortable mixture of servility and complacency as the legal heir of the estate. Only her father could extract amusement from this. As it happened, the Darcys were strongly pressed to visit Rosings, but neither of them felt that Lady Catherine's grudging acceptance of Elizabeth required this degree of sacrifice in the near future. Reminding herself that Longbourn would ultimately be Charlotte's home, Elizabeth decided her friend could not reasonably look for any further assistance from a member of the Bennet family.

These concerns were trivial compared with news Darcy received, which could not be confided to his wife until he joined her after she had gone upstairs to rest. He began slowly and reluctantly.

"Henry Fitzwilliam is to be invalided out."

Surprised by his tone, Elizabeth urged, "But this is good news, my dear; your cousin has suffered enough battles, and recurring fevers endured in the Peninsula are ruining his health. Lady Otterburn will be glad to have her son back in England - and I had the impression he was thinking of marriage."

"You are correct. He means soon to announce his engagement, and hopes for our good wishes despite his parents' threat not to receive his wife should the marriage take place. This may be a warning burst of anger, hoping he has not yet committed himself, for his choice is a grave affront to their family pride. I have met her, and you know of her; the Miss Higgins who arranged those additional comforts for Henry's regiment."

Elizabeth was confused.

"The tradesman's daughter who has both the money and the organising ability? But didn't you describe her as middle-aged, astute in business matters but socially unpresentable?"

"Just so," agreed her husband, his forbidding expression reminding her of the early days of their acquaintance. "I concede that Miss Higgins possesses a clever mind but it has not been improved by education as I understand the word. She is not a lady, has no claims to beauty or birth, is past her youth, but might not be past childbearing. Higgins is a local name in the Otterburn area - respectable people, not usually aiming to rise above their class. This particular Miss Higgins' outstanding intelligence made her a favoured protégée of the Countess. Naturally the whole relationship was based on both sides accepting the impassable gulf between them, so the Otterburns' disapproval is bitterly intensified."

Elizabeth's twinge of sympathy for the Otterburns was immediately challenged by remembering that her Uncle Gardiner – deservedly loved and respected by Darcy – also earned his living in trade. This apparent similarity was overcome by the fact that Mr Gardiner was a merchant, not a shopkeeper. Miss Higgins belonged firmly in the latter category, but (other circumstances being favourable) in the eyes of the world great wealth tended to minimise the stain of low-birth.

On further thought Elizabeth leaned towards the notion that if all Miss Higgins lacked was a little polish, surely *that* could be more easily corrected than the gross defects of character displayed by both the Earl and his heir. But the difficulty of the local connection in Otterburn would always remain.

Darcy silently proffered the letter, and while she read it thought of the of the way of life he and Elizabeth meant to create around Pemberley; ideally it would involve not only their children, but friends who shared their attitudes and concerns. It was a misfortune that the neighbouring families of appropriate rank had never become his intimates. Their diversity ranged from patterns of virtue to frivolous libertines but unfortunately their only commonly shared qualities, were (according to the elder Darcys) lack of sensitivity and intellect. Their young son, by nature inclined to share his parents' feelings of superiority, was increasingly lonely as he grew up.

Now there was an encouraging enlargement in the number of friends reasonably nearby. Several recent acquaintances were due to the Bingleys. Admittedly their standards were less rigorous than his, but it was encouraging that their particular favourites, the Jeffersons, were already known by repute through connections in the Pemberley area. Then there was Gervase, like the Bingleys, not more than thirty miles away.

A few years earlier Darcy had pre-determined Colonel Fitzwilliam's future when he retired from the army. The tenancy of an attractive small estate scarcely ten miles away was to be bestowed on this life-long friend in an arrangement highly beneficial to them both. Despite

Henry's own fortunes amounting to little more than his army pension, Pemberley's owner knew his cousin possessed a sympathetic understanding of the serious obligations imposed by rank and wealth. Darcy's high-handedness about organising other people's lives without consulting them, on this occasion was reinforced by a genuine delicacy about playing the role of a benefactor to whom thanks might be owed. Thus the Colonel, amazingly enough, had never heard of these arrangements for his future benefit.

Now they would all be negated, for the rich wife would be able to buy her husband a large property, possibly far removed from Derbyshire. Too generous to begrudge such a worthy man his own sphere of influence Darcy tried to persuade himself that discussing their separate problems would be of equal benefit, but knew that such a situation would fall far below his previous expectations. The end of the Napoleonic Wars would bring home innumerable newly discharged soldiers with scant chance of employment and therefore ripe for lawless violence. Justice and compassion demanded that destitute men be offered work, but not to the detriment of disciplined order. Here the Colonel could have provided invaluable guidance.

Despite his disastrous interference between Bingley and Jane Bennet, Darcy had not yet entirely repressed the wish to influence his friends' matrimonial choices. His instinctive disapproval of Gervase choosing to marry a governess had been overcome by the intelligence and fortitude of Mrs Gervase and her sisters. Their homely, unpretentious manners, if still a matter of regret, were no longer found offensive. But it created a vastly different situation when Henry Fitzwilliam, his father an Earl, his mother belonging to one of the most illustrious families in England, proposed to marry a shop-keeper's daughter whose undoubted philanthropy might be dangerously mixed with egalitarianism. Darcy even foresaw that, despite her obvious social deficiencies, she might be opinionated enough to reject guidance.

Radical change had already forced its way into the world he hoped to control, but setting aside these misgivings, Darcy decided that once the marriage took place that low-born woman must be received at Pemberley. The sympathetic tones in which Elizabeth was now speaking assured him of her support.

"He writes of deep respect, strong commitment, if not as a man deeply in love."

"Such feelings would not be possible in this case."

Man and wife exchanged a lovingly complacent glance, before Elizabeth continued.

"But he deserves better, as you understand more fully than I do. He would not, would he, marry purely for money, as Charlotte Collins so shockingly did? There is respect and gratitude I think."

"There are degrees of prudence in marriage. My cousin must pay some attention to fortune when he chooses a wife, but he offers not only social consequence, but admirable personal qualities. Undoubtedly there must be a number of educated, high-principled, gentlewomen with reasonable fortunes, despite that memorable argument at Netherfield when I claimed that few women..."

"Fewer than six," prompted his wife, smiling.

"I admit to being in a captious mood, not unconnected with your disturbing presence, my dear, and that evening only eligible young women were being discussed - a requirement Fitzwilliam obviously feels able to forego. Miss Higgins cannot properly be described as a lady. It is beyond belief."

"Rosings!" Elizabeth suddenly recollected. "Charlotte's letter mentioned that the Colonel was expected there. Will her ladyship try to interfere with this engagement?"

"Unlike her previous attempt to meddle in the concerns of a nephew, interference in this case might almost be warranted. But where an affectionate mother fails there is no hope for the bullying tactics of an aunt. I half wish he were visiting Pemberley instead of Rosings, but a man who has pledged himself must not be argued with."

Colonel Fitzwilliam did not propose a visit to the Darcys, but his mother did, sending an express message to ask if it would be convenient for her to arrive within the next few days. Mrs Bennet was half inclined to delay her departure for Dufton in order to meet this aristocratic connection, but finally decided that as the Countess was reckoned a 'blue stocking' she would be better left to Mr Bennet. This brought immeasurable relief to Elizabeth who dreaded an encounter between two women so completely different; one given to endless empty chatter, the other to unembarrassed silence broken by plain, unaffected, sensible speech. In all likelihood Darcy's aunt would have offered no reply – other than an impenetrable look - to Mrs Bennet's inanities, thus inducing an even greater flood of words.

During the first visit of the Otterburns, Darcy had been delighted to observe a high degree of mutual respect and affection developing between his wife and his aunt, despite the latter's usual prejudices in favour of aristocratic birth. Elizabeth's engaging manners and strong mind appealed to the Countess, but it was impossible that a similar concession would ever be extended to a local tradesman's daughter notably lacking in social graces. The best he could hope (and it was a faint hope mainly centred on some future year when anger might have cooled) was that, for Henry's sake, the family would meet with a moderate appearance of good will anywhere but at Otterburn Castle; or that at least his mother would follow this policy.

Even as his wife's sense of reason brought her close to Darcy's pessimistic view, her feelings argued against it, making her deeply reluctant to have any part in pronouncements about the marriage. Fortunately it was more than likely Lady Otterburn wished to confer only with her nephew, while Elizabeth could properly claim the need to give her father whatever time she could spare from Cecilia.

The Countess stayed only three nights, admired the baby, wished to protect the young mother's health and spirits, but inevitably brought sadness with her. It was some consolation for Elizabeth to observe that her ladyship and Mr Bennet immediately appreciated each other, his whimsical humour providing an amusing contrast to her brief yet pertinent observations. Listening to their conversation, Elizabeth, who had never seen her father appear to greater advantage, sorrowed for what he had lost by youthful misjudgement.

To her nephew and his wife, the Countess announced that if her son married Miss Higgins his family could never receive them at Otterburn, and would strive to avoid encountering them anywhere else. She chose not to expand on that point. Would there be a public snub, wondered Elizabeth, or a minimal acknowledgement to defuse gossip? Before Darcy could explain his own attitude, his aunt maintained there was a chance that Miss Higgins had not yet received a formal proposal. Thus Lady Catherine had got him down to Rosings under the unlikely pretext she needed to consult him.

"Measure our desperation, that we welcomed her involvement knowing that at least she isn't trying to make a match for her sickly girl, that being an obsession solely connected with you, Darcy, as the son of her beloved sister. Other possibilities were mentioned; presumably they do not include Mrs Cartwright who is among the guests. She is scarcely older than the Higgins woman, but our families have been acquainted for decades; if there was any mutual attraction it would have declared itself before now."

The name Cartwright in this connection so alarmed Lady Otterburn's listeners they but half attended as her remarks continued.

"The de Bourgh crude tactics are unlikely to work with Henry, but at least he is briefly removed from that woman. With that same purpose in view I hope you people might consider getting him to Pemberley."

"He has informed us of his commitment," said Darcy, "so we cannot invite him as if he were unattached. Of course there is no impropriety in his visiting us alone, but I believe my cousin will expect assurances that, when he marries, his wife will be received here. Although I share your disapproval, Elizabeth and I have decided to accept his choice. I am sorry if this pains you."

"It may upset my husband and eldest son, but, Darcy, you completely misunderstand my feelings. *We* have no alternative, but Henry should not forfeit all his friends. I still hope the match may be prevented, but if it takes place I am glad his cousins will be loyal to him."

Her feelings always under strong control, the Countess managed to continue without apparent distress.

"It must be clear to everyone that my younger son is in every way superior to my elder, but Haslett is the heir, and has married a woman of birth and fortune who, it is to be hoped, will produce children. Haslett is a spendthrift and a womaniser, but she will be faithful, though heaven knows she is a silly little creature. Now we will speak no more of these things, but rejoin Mr Bennet and Georgiana who may welcome additional company."

Elizabeth made a polite gesture of assent before leading the way, her thoughts a confusion of disbelief and disapproval. No hint of future reconciliation was offered. Lady Otterburn appeared ready to cast off the one admirable member of her family because he was marrying beneath himself, yet could still endure a husband and elder son who had nothing but their rank to commend them. Knowing of the particularly warm attachment between the younger son and his mother she found the decision beyond comprehension.

The Countess, solicitous for Elizabeth's welfare, made a rare request for music, thus keeping Georgiana busy at the piano for the remainder of the evening and allowing her sister and aunt to sit together on a sofa with little need for conversation. While only too anxious 'to speak no more of these things' Elizabeth's unsuccessful efforts to banish the subject from her thoughts left her thoroughly dispirited, producing a sudden access of irritation about the formalities of life at Pemberley which prevented her soothing her spirits in the way that most appealed to her. She would have liked to spend her time in the nursery, even if it meant just sitting beside the baby's cradle, but how could she suddenly explain the need for more than a routine visit?

In her present humour, trivial restrictions imposed by a fixed hierarchy, seemed dangerous examples of the rigid code of manners that had caused Lady Otterburn to separate herself from a loved and loving son, whose actions impugned his social discretion rather than his honour. Elizabeth was in no mood to admit the argument that, given the particular circumstances of everyone involved, his choice of Miss Higgins offered an almost unbearable insult to his parents.

The evening ended early. Darcy, not yet aware of the extent of his wife's feelings, escorted her to their apartments before continuing with his aunt to her dressing room for a final word. Elizabeth, seeking solitude, dismissed her maid, then struggled awkwardly to remove a hair ornament which had been troubling her all evening, with the unfortunate result that just as Darcy arrived, an unreasonably hard tug entangled it further, bringing to her eyes the tears hitherto so carefully restrained. It was mortifying to give her husband cause for anxiety when by all reasonable standards her health was fully restored. Ingrained in Darcy's character was a chivalrous instinct to protect – it might be said, to control – his womenfolk, thus he was alert (overly alert thought Elizabeth) to any weakness she betrayed.

"I promise you I am entirely well my dear; this has nothing to do with my health, and everything to do with a simple matter of tangled hair, combined with inescapable agitation about Lady Otterburn and Colonel Fitzwilliam. You may feel I am too readily upset, but this was caused by a combination of circumstances. Truthfully, the tears began only when I tried to release my hair from this ornament."

His reasonable suggestion (even as she dried her eyes and he set about removing the offending jewel) that her maid should have been in attendance, brought this reply:

"Tonight I had no wish to summon Rebecca. Just at the moment I feel, irrationally, that the relationship with servants is part of a system that disallows the needs of the individual."

To this rather wild claim, her husband responded with, "I say no more about the absence of your maid, my dear, since we often choose to be free of attendants when going to bed, but isn't it somewhat unreasonable to link the Otterburns' family quarrel to the overpowering presence of servants?"

"Not as a primary cause of course. Rebelling against the inevitably formal structures in our life was a relief after finding myself deeply shocked by the rigid attitudes of an admired friend. I still had a false hope that the particular excellencies of Colonel Fitzwilliam would soften your aunt's adamant reaction.

"Disappointment made me desperate to get away briefly from the adherence, not to principles, but to stupid rules with which I cannot agree. I thought of sitting in the nursery beside Cecilia, but Nurse would need explanations and reassurances, making what should be natural and easy, tiresomely difficult. Sometimes it seems the domination of servants over us is as great as our domination over them. Either way it felt intolerable to me tonight."

The look of increasing anxiety on her husband's face made Elizabeth ashamed of her unwarranted self-absorption. She hastened to say, "Dear Darcy, forgive this foolish mood. It is inexcusable to be indulging selfish feelings to this extent when you have much greater cause to be upset. Your attachment to your aunt and cousin, having lasted all your life, must be immeasurably stronger than mine; what is your response to this sad decision? Tell me *your* feelings; do you hope for any compromise or do you believe the Otterburns will maintain an absolute breach?"

As gratified by these affectionate words as he had been alarmed by the preceding outburst, her husband concentrated on voicing some of his chaotic feelings.

"It must be accounted shameful for a younger son of an Earl to form an alliance with the daughter of a tradesman, particularly a local tradesman. It creates an impossible situation. The structure of our society simply does not allow for this - regardless of the probity of many individual shopkeepers - and I hasten to say Miss Higgins is unassailable in that regard.

"That is my general view, but obviously new criteria must be invoked in special cases. The painful truth is that my uncle and elder cousin are inferior to Miss Higgins in intelligence and integrity. She is ill bred, they are well bred and I do consider breeding important – but it cannot, must not, be considered of paramount importance when duty and principle are lacking. Only my aunt and my younger cousin have consistently upheld the family honour."

Darcy fell silent, embarrassed to engage Elizabeth in a discussion about unsuitable alliances considering the fact that his first proposal of marriage had included an outspoken condemnation of *her* family. Fortunately, the resemblance did not go far. However vulgar the behaviour of some of the Bennets, there remained a measurable social distance between them and the Higgins – nor did they live in the environs of Pemberley!

For the same reason Elizabeth was also momentarily silenced, recalling Darcy's early objections to her mother's noisy lack of restraint and the unformed manners of Mary, Kitty and Lydia. In the event, the difficulties following their marriage had not been extreme, for only Kitty was a frequent visitor, and she was steadily improving in manners if not in mind. Moreover, the final reassurance was that they were undeniably the wife and daughters of a gentleman - a status denied to Miss Higgins.

Naturally, both Darcys preferred to concentrate on the current dilemma. Elizabeth began, "I am increasingly drawn to Miss Higgins who has great natural advantages to offset her lack of social ones. She probably fails most of the criteria Caroline Bingley required of an accomplished woman: music, singing, dancing, drawing, the correct air and mode of expression. But while they add to the pleasures of social life, you have particularly criticized female education for concentrating on a trivial smattering of these attributes."

Her husband, anxious to agree that Miss Higgins had made good use of her natural gifts, perhaps spoke of her more favourably than he had intended.

"When making my point about the degradation such an unequal union inflicts on the entire family, remember that I was speaking generally. The excellent – super excellent – character of Fitzwilliam, requires me to accept his choice, a decision further strengthened by the incontrovertible fact that Miss Higgins devotes a major part of her time, money, and intellectual abilities, to the welfare of others. My aunt knows that morally and mentally Miss Higgins is undoubtedly superior to the Earl and his heir. Unfortunately that cannot alter the fact that most of her adult life was spent as a draper's assistant who never aspired to refinements of manner. I might argue that fake gentility is even more abhorrent, but when she was supervising provisions for Henry's troops I found her loud, opinionated, overbearing."

He suddenly smiled.

"I seem to be offering an accurate description of Lady Catherine, but the world is unjust enough to tolerate that in a woman surrounded by the trappings of aristocracy. It is not a suitable demeanour for a draper's daughter trying to make herself acceptable to society.

"The cynical truth is, it would be easier if only she had appeared from somewhere abroad, complete with her wealth, her natural gifts, and a smattering of polish disguising her actual origins. Miss Higgins' background cannot be disguised, nor does she attempt to disguise it, being defiantly aware of her superior abilities."

"Though my respect for her increases," replied Elizabeth, "alas, how can the Otterburns ever be reconciled? If only she could subdue her aggressive instincts. But I conclude they are an inextricable part of her high achievements."

"The saddest thing," said Darcy, "is that the Countess is as obdurate as the Earl. She accuses Henry of disloyalty by allowing his mother to be insulted by one who had received particular kindnesses from her."

"Insulted?" said Elizabeth doubtfully, "Your aunt's words are always carefully chosen, but surely Colonel Fitzwilliam does not consider such an accusation justified? Has Miss Higgins by any chance actually made derogatory comments?"

"I would consider that most unlikely. It is more likely to be a misunderstanding. The Countess would be ready to find her late protégée's current actions a personal affront, and the gratitude and esteem she *assumes* Miss Higgins to have felt, may not perhaps have reached the unqualified heights expected by her benefactor. In short, Miss Higgins may have used words, which if not entirely adulatory seemed reasonable enough to her."

"Is it possible," suggested Elizabeth "they may reach a patched up agreement whereby the Henry Fitzwilliams are never in Otterburn, but the two couples manage a reasonable civility when they meet on neutral ground? Perhaps the greatest service we can render your cousin is to entertain them here?"

Darcy's reply was not encouraging.

"Unlikely – but possibly in the course of time. But at the moment my greatest wish is to put aside these anxieties for the remainder of the night and reclaim our own personal life."

❧❧

Scene Eight

❧❧

Elizabeth slept better than she had expected, but before she met her aunt in the morning the wearyingly familiar arguments returned. Nor did there seem any escape, for following Lady Otterburn's departure, Georgiana's need to discuss this problem overcame a habitual reluctance to criticize other members of her family.

"How can my aunt do this to her son? You know he is one of my guardians, and on all occasions has been so kind and attentive. Being sixteen years my senior I regarded him rather as an uncle, until his last visit here when he treated me as a friend rather than a ward. He is not as outstanding as our Fitzwilliam (how awkward these names are) but truly good, and Miss Higgins' work proves her worth, despite other problems difficult to overcome. It is true her speech is a little..."

"You have met her?"

"Yes, by chance. Mrs Annesley and I were driving in the Park and we saw the Colonel ahead of us. Just for a moment I thought he was with his mother, for Miss Higgins shares her height and..." Georgiana sought appropriate words, "a certain unstudied way of moving. When we met, that slight resemblance was increased by her way of dispensing with formalities just as my aunt does. I do find it strange that the Otterburns specifically criticize her manner and deportment as unladylike. And although the Northern accent is noticeable her voice has a reasonably agreeable tone."

"An agreeable tone?" Elizabeth was surprised, "Not loud and commanding?"

"Well perhaps there was an air of certainty, but why not – she is a woman of mature age. As the few sentences she spoke were mainly addressed to me, any trace of deference would have been unpleasant for us all."

Georgiana's natural diffidence did not preclude an acceptance of her own privileged place in the world, but a Miss Higgins presented to her by her cousin was not to be treated as a representative of 'Higgins & Company, Quality Drapers.'

Her thoughts generally confused, Elizabeth sounded facetious rather than serious.

"A woman of her intelligence and confidence could get rid of the accent, leaving the uninitiated to think Henry Fitzwilliam is marrying some distant relative of his mother's family."

Georgiana, finding she could not approve of this, tried to modify her words while Elizabeth amused herself by making Miss Higgins the natural child of some nobleman. Would that increase or diminish her standing? She now felt a positive wish to meet Miss Higgins and wished their cousin would bring her to Pemberley, where at least she would be considered a more acceptable choice than Mrs Cartwright. Despite Darcy's criticism, a truly coarse woman would not have been acceptable to the Colonel whatever the combined power of her intellect and fortune.

A smaller, but immediately compelling, problem now absorbed all her attention. Nurse, having just placed Cecilia in her mother's arms, was describing two wakeful periods in the night when baby seemed fretful and colicky, but fortunately settled fairly soon. With some embarrassment at her own inconsistencies,

Elizabeth felt all the usefulness of experienced servants. How reassuring to be able to rely on a nurse who could judge the difference between a minor and a major upset, and could be relied upon to waken the mother only in the latter event.

Turning her eyes from Cecilia, she saw two figures through the window.

"Georgiana, would you ring the nursery bell? Cecilia must come downstairs to greet her Papa and Grandpapa, and the bay window in the library will be the very place to catch their attention."

No one approved. Georgiana feared her brother would expect her to prevent this unusual action, and Nurse wanted the baby to be changed into finer clothes, but as Elizabeth accepted no delay the whole party quickly arrived at the library window. A footman was dispatched to alert the men, who now included Mr Warriner. As they approached, the young women smiled out at them, one more merrily than the other, but the baby was a mere bundle of shawls until Elizabeth turned around allowing Miss Cecilia Darcy to gaze earnestly across her mother's shoulder. I know it is too soon, thought Darcy, but that little face looks almost sentient. In spite of Elizabeth's awkwardly twisted head it was an engaging tableau, and Mr Warriner stepped up to the window and greeted the baby by flattening his nose against the glass. Cecilia's forehead wrinkled and her fingers tightened on her mother's hair; this meant nothing of course, but everyone was delighted, especially Elizabeth, who was usually irritated by Mr Warriner's childish affectations, but now decided to agree with her father that these were follies to be enjoyed.

It was Mr Bennet's habit to restrain his quixotic speech in Darcy's presence, assuring his daughter that he stood in too much awe of her husband to be flippant. This in itself was flippant. It was entirely foreign to Mr Bennet's nature to offer anyone such a high degree of respect, but genuine feelings of gratitude to this son-in-law for appreciating Lizzy's qualities made him unusually forbearing. Only when father and daughter were alone did he offer his satirical views of the people around him, while omitting comments on her husband whose stately manners he not infrequently found amusing rather than impressive. Lady Otterburn's company was more completely to his taste, as she proved clever enough to be admired, in addition to entertaining him by her downright address. Learning that her son was about to make an unacceptable marriage, he asked Lizzy if the woman in question managed to be as impudently flattering as Lydia's worthless husband.

"Entirely the reverse I believe, sir. She is the heiress of a family of shopkeepers, and her inferior birth is not disguised by the appealing manners of a George Wickham. The lack of appropriate polish is an additional irritant."

"A strange objection from a woman whose own behaviour shows a lack of concern for social graces. But I already forestall you, Lizzy; an aristocrat may dispense with forms that other people must observe. Yet I still approve of the Countess. Why should she connect herself with tradesmen? Even in our more modest lives we suffer from vulgar connections."

This rather unseemly reference to his wife's family in Meryton was quickly softened by unqualified praise of Mr and Mrs Gardiner, before Elizabeth continued.

"Darcy concedes that Miss Higgins is both capable and intelligent; clearly what she lacks is any elegance of mind and manner. Georgiana, in her milder way, said much the same."

"They have both met her? I envy them. When Lady Otterburn leaves perhaps the Colonel will bring Miss Higgins here; she would provide an intriguing contrast to Warriner who is also intelligent but chooses to appear incapable of managing daily life."

"His inanities are more noticeable in your presence, for you enjoy leading him on, whereas Darcy has a inhibiting effect."

"Your husband does not share our taste for oddities of behaviour, but Warriner, I deduce, is a man of sense, who has found a satisfactory way to evade tedious duties. The material needs of his parishioners are already supplied, there is no call for him as a domestic chaplain and his sermons are admirably short, leaving him plenty of time to pursue Natural History. With a manservant in addition to his housekeeper, he leads a more pampered, if less luxurious, life than the Master and Mistress of Pemberley. It all depends on his remaining unmarried - though to certain young women he may appear beguiling rather than foolish."

Elizabeth did not mention her need for a Mrs Warriner to oversee the Sunday schools and their teachers, contenting herself with: "Darcy agrees with you he is unlikely to marry."

"Very probably; but I would have you note a degree of sympathetic ease between him and Miss Darcy. Now she is also worthy of study. When she ventures to speak her own views rather than her brother's she shows the makings of a thoughtful woman, but I can scarcely blame her for being overawed by Darcy, when I have admitted to being in the same position. She may learn to be bolder by watching you, Lizzy. Your mother assured me Miss Darcy was destined for Colonel Fitzwilliam, but now he has settled on a different heiress there may be a chance for Warriner - if your husband would countenance so modest a union for his sister. It would at least keep her at Pemberley."

Elizabeth doubted if marriage with the Colonel was ever projected.

"He has been more like an uncle than a cousin. With her fortune in addition to her talents, Georgiana will not lack suitors, but she needs greater confidence in order to choose wisely. This continuing diffidence makes her prefer the company of unassuming people - which clearly applies to Mr Warriner without implying any romantic attachment."

Mr Bennet was easily persuaded to share her views after she described the calm friendship between Georgiana and Dominic Cartwright, who must be reckoned an infinitely more eligible character.

"This shall be lesson to me to leave matchmaking to Mrs Bennet, who has her hands full enough with Mary and Kitty. I shall advise them to concentrate on hunting for husbands among the Bingleys' friends instead of coming here to compete with Miss Darcy, who has the unfair advantage of character as well as fortune."

Precisely because these comments mirrored her own thoughts, they were very unwelcome to Elizabeth. How could her father so cheerfully admit the inferiority of his daughters, when he had greatly contributed to it by his own neglect? She and Jane had not suffered as greatly as their sisters. For the two firstborn Mr Bennet had felt the natural instinct of affection - which flourished when the years proved them to be free of their mother's invincible triviality and uncertain temper. It might have seemed that Mary, the third child, most closely resembled her father, but where he was quickwitted and satirical, she was slow and dull. He mocked all her solemn attempts to be well read, although more direction and encouragement from him might have helped her avoid those wearisome public displays of platitudes. The last two girls he left entirely to their mother.

Elizabeth loved her father, but the older she grew the less she was able to respect him. It was a painful combination. To escape these feelings she was surprisingly willing to turn her thoughts to the Cartwrights. The son continued to correspond with Georgiana and Mrs Annesley, but now travel in Europe was increasingly feasible; his recent letters were full of plans likely to keep him away for years. This would complete the break with Mrs Cartwright without making Georgiana wonder at her brother's antipathy to both mother and son.

During the next few weeks Georgiana visited the Bingleys at Dufton Hall, where her friend Caroline Bingley was also a guest. It was a flattering proof of Mr Bennet's esteem that he not only suggested travelling with her, but absolutely kept this engagement while remaining elusive about the rest of his plans. It so happened that he returned to Pemberley within a few days, with comments that tantalised by saying both more and less than his daughter expected. The intriguing fact that Miss Bingley had been at Rosings prior to her arrival at Dufton was almost overlooked by Mr Bennet, but with typical indifference to a daughter's future welfare he mockingly reported on Kitty's brief romance with an eligible clergyman. At first the gentleman was encouragingly attentive, but when the overpowering attentions of Mrs Bennet were added to those of her daughter, he showed signs of alarm. Jane was able to exert a moderating influence on her sister, but her mother was impervious to gentle advice.

"I suggested stronger words from Bingley, including a hint that his own courtship had faltered under her energetic attempts to facilitate it - but with no hope of any such action from either Jane or her husband. It is doubtful the young man will declare himself in the next few days, if at all, so I decided to return here for my last week. It can be argued that a life-long union should not be decided after a few social encounters, but would another month or two provide significant new insights?"

"This comes close to Charlotte Collins' view of matrimony."

"While she was still Charlotte Lucas I respected her good sense, but now she has become Mrs Collins I am no longer flattered to find we think alike."

Before the dressing-bell Elizabeth and Darcy sat together in their Chinese room. In all the vastness of Pemberley this was the only sitting room where he would discard a jacket or in any other way relax his formal attire. Elizabeth's obvious approval of this informality, caused Darcy to ask for a reason.

"You well know how much I enjoy a daytime hour alone with you, free of conversational restraints, but I am curious to know why removing my coat, or changing into slippers... "

"That extensive collection embroidered by any number of enthusiastic young ladies, who should be grateful to me for persuading you to use them."

"We will take their gratitude for granted while I finish my question. Why is this an important concession when we have the pleasure of retiring to bed together every night?" His wife's quizzical look made him concede a difference, but, taking pleasure in the conversation, he added, "As for the comfortable domesticity implied by some degree of undress, remember how frequently I come to your dressing-room."

"Georgiana, or Jane, might also be there, in addition to my maid being frequently about. And the concluding argument, my dear, is that in my dressing-room I am the one not fully dressed, making me look frivolous compared with your imposing presence. Your advantage in size is unalterable, but clothes also carry important messages and sometimes I enjoy seeing your appearance match your relaxed mood. Perhaps I am a Delilah, attacking your armour instead of your hair; but have no fear, the impulse springs not from revenge but love."

Even as he decried everything but the final words as nonsense, he knew her 'nonsense' was partially if not entirely true. Rejecting the peacock fashions available to men, he chose to have his natural hauteur emphasised by meticulous tailoring in sombre colours, whereas Elizabeth (even with a lavish increase in personal money) remained loyal to a softness and freedom of movement suited to her youthful appearance. He wanted no change in her, but she hoped for a slight relaxation from a style of dress which, allied to his natural gravity, made him appear more than six years her senior.

Content with her words and her glance, he changed the subject.

"As Caroline Bingley has rejected her recent suitor, Mr Forbes, perhaps Lady Catherine was offering her as a bait to Fitzwilliam. Though far from ideal she must be reckoned an improvement upon Miss Higgins."

"I was not aware that your aunt knew Miss Bingley."

"They would be likely to encounter each other in London. Caroline would obviously appreciate an invitation to Rosings, and I admit the possibility of such a match had occurred to me before her artifice and ambition became increasingly apparent. Spending so much time alone with the family group at Netherfield made me realise how entirely Bingley's sisters lack his open nature. However, as the engagement to Miss Higgins is even now being published, all this is irrelevant."

Recognising that his wife's smile alluded to Miss Bingley's assiduous attentions to himself, he did not identify yet another reason for her amusement - his calm conviction that an invitation to Rosings would be generally sought after, disregarding the fact that his sole pleasure in visits to his aunt was the knowledge of family duty fulfilled. Elizabeth, however, shared his belief that Miss Bingley would find the honour of being Lady Catherine's guest enough to nullify the boredom.

When Georgiana returned she brought a scribbled note from Jane, which she allowed Elizabeth to read in silence before making her own comment. Jane apologized for great haste in writing, but managed to include a great deal of information.

Once Kitty stops seeking instant romance her good qualities will procure steadier suitors. There is no need for the rather unbecoming air of anxious hurry possibly induced by our dear mother's feelings.

Through Georgiana we had the pleasure of meeting the Gervase family, who were persuaded to come to Dufton for a night; or more accurately, the women of the family stayed, while Mr Gervase returned the same day to spare his mother having only the servants for company. What a truly excellent man he is, and how gratified Darcy must be to have settled his friend at Kympton.

Charles, as agreed, has leased the house in Lyme, still a quiet seaside resort despite its elegant new Assembly Rooms. Details will follow, but this house should be the ideal choice to share for the summer -

close to the harbour yet with spacious private grounds commanding views of the cliffs and seashore. Many half-pay Naval officers and their families have lodgings in town but Charles sends personal assurances to you, Lizzie, that there are no military encampments! I shall be sorry to leave all the pleasures of my new home, but the seaside and the company of dear Lizzie and her family are inducement enough. The long journey (so much further from Pemberley than Scarborough) should be amply rewarded by the milder climate of the south west coast.

In discussing this letter with her husband, Elizabeth left his sister to report on the Gervase family, including the fact that Mr Warriner had been at Kympton - to visit his clerical colleague, Darcy supposed, but Georgiana quietly offered another explanation – Mr Warriner needed to discuss alterations to a set of botanical drawings Maria Porter was doing for him. His requirements were stringent in contrast to his usual vagueness. These were by no means the first corrections. This anecdote supported Elizabeth's view that the young man's air of unworldly incompetence masked a determination to accept the assistance willingly offered by young women while giving little in return. Maria, who might have felt singled out for attention, now probably understood that the disarming manners were bestowed on everyone, and sprang more from general indifference than universal benevolence.

These musings were banished by the next piece of news which concerned an unexpected, yet apparently vigorous, love. Accompanying Colonel Fitzwilliam to Rosings, was his senior officer, General Tollington, who was known to be in pursuit of Mrs Cartwright and was continuing what appeared to be a successful courtship. According to Caroline Bingley it was likely the two marriages would be celebrated at the same time, possibly at the General's family place somewhere in the south or west of England. As the two ladies were tolerably well acquainted, a double wedding placed the beleaguered Colonel and Miss Higgins safely among friends.

Lady Catherine, belatedly realising that Mrs Cartwright had acted as mentor to Miss Higgins concerning dress and manners, accused her of treachery to her class, and to her hostess in particular. It was an awkward moment; the General was outraged, but Mrs Cartwright pleaded the allowances due to Lady Catherine's age, rank, and personal idiosyncrasies - a sycophantic view supported by Caroline Bingley.

Both Darcys were engaged by the same thought; for Mrs Cartwright to remarry was indeed the best way for her to vanish from their lives. Notwithstanding the close friendship between Fitzwilliam and Tollington there was no need for the latter to be invited to Pemberley, and it was in Derbyshire, when the expedition to Lyme was over, that Elizabeth expected to meet the new Mrs Fitzwilliam.

This expectation proved entirely unfounded. Accompanied by Cecilia and appropriate servants, the Darcys began their leisurely progress southwest, visiting friends and family connections. At Bath, a letter forwarded from their cousin mentioned some advance in the wedding date, as Dominic Cartwright's ship might sail any day. Georgiana (who was already staying in Bath) chose this occasion to remind her brother.

"Do you recall suggesting a Continental Tour once the war was over? But now you and Elizabeth are parents, perhaps foreign travel will not attract you in the near future?"

"I hope that for some time England will satisfy Elizabeth's delight in new scenes," replied Darcy. "Before marrying she had rarely been far from home, so is longing to see more of the natural beauties of her native land, and the great monuments man has raised upon it. This need not deter you, Georgiana; next year it should be possible for you and Mrs Annesley to travel with suitable escorts."

Accepting this as a general suggestion, Georgiana emphasised (particularly in speaking to Elizabeth, who had just entered the room) how hard it would be to find travelling companions to compare with them. In addition to her brother's erudition, he also possessed the useful ability to command the best horses and the best lodgings; but above all this, her sister's enthusiasm made every experience enjoyable.

Elizabeth was pleased with the compliment.

"I admit, that without leaving these shores I am already greatly excited about seeing the ocean for the first time. And to know that from our house we can watch the waves flinging themselves against cliffs and into chasms. Georgiana are you sure one week at Lyme will be enough for you? I don't believe the other resorts can compete in natural grandeur."

"By being more fully developed they attract people of greater consequence," was her husband's repressive comment.

In Georgiana's absence he spoke of his conviction that Cartwright posed no threat to her happiness, and with her general improvement in confidence this was the moment for her to meet as many suitable people as possible. He was suddenly aware that even the hint of a mild liking for Warriner was too much. Freshly reminded of the sharpness of his observation, Elizabeth, believing the danger was close to nonexistent, could not resist the teasing remark that Warriner's well-proportioned figure contrasted favourably with Cartwright's appearance.

Darcy was not amused.

"By visiting the more fashionable watering-places it is to be hoped she will meet men of family and fortune, with notable presence and natural vigour of mind and body. Warriner lacks not only fortune but proper manliness; we shall say no more about him."

Half-wishing her flippant remark unsaid, Elizabeth returned to Colonel Fitzwilliam's letter, complaining that the fold obscured the exact location of Tollington Court. It was a complete surprise to learn the full address named a village less than thirty miles from Lyme, which the Darcys would reach just too late for the wedding. The Colonel had no forewarning that his cousins' summer plans would bring them into his neighbourhood, making Darcy wonder if, by riding ahead of his family, he would be a welcome guest? There were two strong arguments against the plan - the double ceremony was to be in the Tollingtons' family chapel, and he would be witnessing not only the wedding vows of his cousin, but of his ex-mistress.

The last fact was decisive. They would continue their unhurried journey, enjoying the welcome extended by their hosts, some of whom lived very retired lives. When planning the route, Elizabeth was relieved her mother had claimed no connections with Dorset, had never heard any good of it, was sure it was inferior to Hertfordshire, and none of its resorts the equal of Brighton. Her father had answered in a different vein; yes he had a distant cousin thereabouts - not seen since they were both young - remembered as a disreputable, but clever, scamp; or on second thoughts was he to be recalled as a stupid fellow and consequently a pillar of the community? It was obviously a fiction, and Mr Bennet's purpose, other than instinctive teasing, uncertain. However, this demolished Elizabeth's slender hope that her father's side of the family might provide her with at least one or two relatives as admirable as the

Gardiners, who, demonstrating the unpredictability of family character, were her mother's kin.

Their West Country hosts, mainly belonging to junior branches of the Darcys or Fitzwilliams, she liked very well. Although far from grand they demonstrated a natural confidence in themselves, but if the isolation of life far from the turnpike roads had produced this independent spirit, was it also responsible for the large numbers of children? Elizabeth hoped no such fate as a child every year for fifteen years or so, awaited her.

Family news was a great staple of conversation, but as none of their relatives knew Colonel Fitzwilliam was in the area (Darcy not choosing to volunteer this information) it was the Inn-keeper, on the last night of their journey, who reported that immediately following yesterday's ceremony both couples had left on extended journeys to unknown destinations. As for the future - Tollington Court was on a long lease to the Colonel who had hired a satisfyingly large number of local people to restore a house that had been long neglected by an impoverished tenant. His bride was fabulously rich, which would be a fine thing for the whole district as well as for General Tollington, whose family, despite their ancient lineage, had always been impoverished. The General, of course, could continue to use the Dower House, but it was believed his lady preferred town life, so they would often be at her London home.

This news could not fail to interest, but Elizabeth was more excited by encountering the sea for the first time. Decorum required her to be sedately seated in the carriage on the steep descent to Lyme when she really wished to hang out of the window and exclaim (as loudly as might her mother or Lydia) at the dramatic glimpses of the sea. The carriage entrance to Lyme Lodge was discouragingly hemmed in by the walls of other properties, but the Bingleys were there to welcome them into the house, and soon she and Jane, with their babies in their arms, stood at the drawing-room windows looking across the lawn to the cliffs and the ocean. Their husbands, able to display their greater knowledge by comparing this view with that of other resorts, fell short of the undiluted pleasure experienced by their wives. However, all four agreed that, allowing for the limitations of temporary lodgings, the two families would be comfortably accommodated. Elizabeth saw Cecilia and her nursemaids settled into the attic rooms they were to share with Edward and his attendants, before exulting in the view from her own bedchamber. Then she had to listen to her maid's worries about the lack of proper dressing rooms. That little closet, also to be used by the valet, would hardly contain more than the bath.

꧁꧂

Scene Nine

꧁꧂

During their first visit to the Circulating Library, the Bingleys had signed the Subscription Book for themselves and the Darcys. Charles felt sure many of the subscribers would provide agreeable company, but put forward no particular plans - a pleasant surprise for Elizabeth whose own wish was to explore the town and its surroundings. She had already accepted the fact that Darcy would be at the livery stables the following day, but was somewhat surprised to learn Charles had business in Weymouth, almost thirty miles away, thus leaving the two young women to occupy themselves. Forewarned of this, the quietly efficient Jane had already organised bathing machines and attendants to start the morning, to be followed by a leisurely stroll through the town afterwards.

The weather was so warm and the bathing so exhilarating that Elizabeth stayed in the water too long for them to be able to reach the Cobb after visiting the library. This was no great hardship as she wanted to share all these new sights with her husband, especially an enticing path winding up the nearest cliff, therefore unlikely to appeal to Jane's more sedentary tastes. Attracted by everything in Lyme, Elizabeth was in no hurry for excursions further afield. Their own garden, in which they sat that evening, provided seclusion while offering glimpses not only of the Cobb and the bay it sheltered, but of a whole range of cliffs stretching from the town. Anxious as she was to explore that nearby path, it was disappointing to learn that in the morning

Darcy would still be busy with horses, and furthermore, discouraged plans for an afternoon excursion. Her disappointment was not assuaged by the argument that, judging by today's weather, the afternoon sun tomorrow might well be too hot for climbing a steep path.

Early the following morning the sun already promised heat, just as Darcy had foreseen. Elizabeth found it strange that Charles had again set off for Weymouth, and even stranger that Jane volunteered no further information. Perhaps she was a little distrait? But a further glance persuaded Elizabeth that Jane's usual calm manner prevailed; the secret could only be a project such as planning an excursion for them all. Charles loved to surprise his friends.

As it happened, their arrangements offered little opportunity for confidential talk, for after visiting the nurseries they went down to the bathing machines, Jane spending only a few minutes in the water while Elizabeth jumped and splashed so vigorously the attendant warned her of over-exertion. Confident of understanding her own constitution, and still slightly provoked that her husband was to be absent all morning, she decided to enjoy the view from that cliff before returning home. Initially Jane urged her to have breakfast before attempting the walk, but was persuaded by the argument that this was possibly the coolest time of day, as indicated by a number of fashionably dressed people already on the lower slopes of the path.

In truth, the air was already becoming humid and her boots proved too light for the deceptively steep climb, but such a panorama of sea and cliffs was finally reached that the discomforts of heat and exertion were forgotten until she turned back towards Lyme, increasingly aware of the sultry heat adding to the stickiness of salt water dried on her skin. For the last mile of footpaths Elizabeth's thoughts were concentrated less on the beauties of nature than on the pleasures of a cool bath and fresh garments, preferably before her husband returned to witness her fatigue.

This feeling was reinforced the moment she reached home, where the long pier glass in the hall showed her bedraggled reflection. How she hoped for an hour with no companion other than Jane. Consequently the two pieces of news that greeted her indoors - that Mrs Bingley had just set off for Weymouth and a Colonel and Mrs Fitzwilliam had called and were strolling in the garden in the hope that she would soon return - caused varying degrees of dismay. Blaming herself for not recognising Jane's anxiety and hoping that Darcy understood more, she sought more information from the Housekeeper.

"Where is my husband; did he accompany my sister to Weymouth?"

"No Madam, he could not instantly be found, and Mrs Bingley was too agitated to wait, though I begged her to do so, and almost immediately the Colonel and his lady arrived. I understand there is a note for you, but Mrs Bingley did not say where she had put it."

Without delay a message was scribbled for Darcy at Upper Lyme, informing him of his cousin's arrival but omitting the worrying news of Jane's precipitate departure. Now she must deal with the Fitzwilliams' ill timed visit. Learning that the housekeeper had already set out refreshments in a shady arbour Elizabeth turned towards the staircase, determined to wash and change while her guests were out of doors, but by ill-chance the Fitzwilliams walked in from the garden even at that moment.

Oppressed by headache and anxiety, she was uncomfortably aware that the sunlight emphasised her crumpled dress and untidy hair. Circumstances to which she would normally react with a laughing apology felt surprisingly hard to bear. However, welcoming the Colonel's bride was of first importance and her own appearance, if not unnoticed would at least go unremarked.

The ladies were introduced, courtesies exchanged, hurried explanations offered on each side but scarcely attended to, when Mrs Fitzwilliam suddenly said, "Mrs Darcy, you are heated and dishevelled; we are unexpected guests who can only be in the way... "

"Pray do not leave," said Elizabeth, politely hiding her displeasure that a stranger should make such an offensively accurate remark. And at a closer glance, this woman, supposedly indifferent to dress, now appeared surprisingly fashionable in her attire. However, a small irritation must not interfere with her wish to make a friend of Mrs Fitzwilliam.

"Within a few minutes I shall rejoin you, and I know my husband will be disappointed if he misses this opportunity to greet you."

"Your baby also seems to be suffering from the heat," added Mrs Fitzwilliam, whose hearing was acute.

"That is young Master Bingley," said the housekeeper, somewhat officiously.

"My nephew is teething," explained Elizabeth, for an unreasonable moment relieved that her formidable guest could not find fault with Cecilia in addition to herself.

After the Colonel had made fond enquiries about his godchild, Elizabeth summoned her maid's assistance to help her change, and also conduct an unsuccessful search for Jane's message. Resigned to wearing a matronly cap to hide her tangled hair, she was quick to rejoin her guests in the cool shade of the arbour, determined not to succumb to the feeling that this woman was, just as Darcy said, entirely ill-bred; the tone, even more than the words, had been decidedly abrasive. Perhaps the fault lay with her; confusion might have made her sound unwelcoming to anyone in the mood to take offence.

This guess was reasonably close to the truth. Matilda Fitzwilliam, well aware that her husband had been greatly attracted by Eliza Bennet before she became Mrs Darcy, was predisposed to see defects in this paragon, for she loved her husband passionately. Yet her jealousy was unwarranted; youth and beauty she lacked, but her ardent affections combined with high principles had won the Colonel's unqualified admiration. While not indifferent to her fortune, his own principles would not have allowed him to make a purely mercenary marriage, and every day in her company increased his esteem. Her mental and physical energies were of vital support to health undermined by a long campaign in which no victory had been won and countless lives lost to fever.

Perhaps it was surprising that a man of the Colonel's discernment occupied the short period of time their hostess was absent by praising her delightful appearance and unaffected charm. It was particularly unfair that Elizabeth, by exerting herself to cover real exhaustion with lively conversation, merely reinforced Mrs Fitzwilliam's opinion that here was a trivial chatterbox undeserving of serious attention.

It may be imagined that several uncomfortable pauses developed. Elizabeth, casting around for an innocuous topic, mentioned the Fitzwilliams' unexpected return home but was sharply corrected; they had never intended a longer absence; who could have informed her otherwise? Embarrassed to admit a gossiping servant as the source, she longed for her husband's return, for although the Colonel conversed valiantly the women remained ill at ease with each other.

All three of them were relieved when Darcy finally appeared. An amused glance at the unfamiliar cap was included in his greeting to his wife, before he offered a heartfelt welcome to Fitzwilliam and his bride - the lady strikingly improved in appearance and address since their last meeting, presumably due to the influence of their mutual acquaintance, Lucy Cartwright Tollington. With caustic approval his wife noted Mrs Fitzwilliam's softened manner, but above all she wanted the guests to depart. She was convinced that her husband was privy to the secret business in Weymouth, though when he enquired about Jane's absence from the group it became apparent he knew nothing of her recent departure. Elizabeth tried to speak lightly.

"She is away from home. While I was climbing the cliffs after bathing this morning, my sister received a message asking her to join Bingley in Weymouth. As the note she left for us has somehow been mislaid, I am sadly ignorant of their plans."

Aware of the distress she was concealing, Darcy still could not allow himself to curtail the hospitality due to a bride, but their cousins, mindful of the journey before them, chose to bring the visit to an end with a pressing invitation to the Darcys and the Bingleys to be their guests at Tollington Court within the next week - which was accepted on condition a return visit to Lyme would follow. All these courtesies seemed intolerably drawn out to Elizabeth, but at last the guests entered their carriage and were waved off.

"Oh how I have wanted you," she burst out.

As Darcy had seen Mrs Fitzwilliam at her most complaisant, he ascribed his wife's agitation entirely to her sister's unexplained trip to Weymouth, combined with physical exhaustion caused by scrambling up cliffs in this oppressive weather. With her usual healthy composure already challenged, how would she react to the truth about Charles Bingley's Weymouth connection? Putting an arm round her as they hurried back into the house, he enquired, "Have you eaten since your exertions this morning - which I consider most imprudent in this heat?"

"No, I sat with our guests but my head ached too much for me to manage food. Trying to welcome them properly while thinking only of Jane, I was so agitated that Mrs Fitzwilliam must have found me a strange creature."

"She is of little account compared with you. Come upstairs; you must eat and rest, but without delay I will tell you as much as I know. Your sister, never suspecting faults in those she loves, has recently accepted the fact that Charles has a natural daughter, now living in Weymouth with her mother. It was a relationship begun in that dismal period after leaving Netherfield, the mother being a young actress supported by Charles ever since."

His wife was speechless, but the expression on her face made him continue quickly.

"My dear love, a few minutes thought will persuade you that the Bingleys, so well suited, so warmly attached, can deal with this crisis, just as we have learned to adjust to a problem stemming from the same period, and not so totally dissimilar."

The presence of a maid bringing refreshments provided Elizabeth with a further chance to reflect in unbroken silence, while her husband settled her comfortably on the chaise longue. Elizabeth's pleasure in receiving these attentions was almost exceeded by her husband's pleasure in offering them, while not altering his decision to protest about that foolhardy walk as soon as she was thoroughly rested. For the moment they spoke only of Bingley's mistress, the relative openness of the discussion somewhat complicated by having to avoid any allusion to Mrs Cartwright. After urging her to sleep, Darcy left the room. Elizabeth was full of concern for her sister. Guileless, guiltless, Jane; what must she feel? How would she bring herself to accept this painful news? Sleep was clearly impossible.

Yet somehow she was unconscious of the heavy rainfall, or the coachman's return from Weymouth, bringing messages from Jane. They were by her side when she woke; the first being the letter that should have remained at Lyme Lodge. This merely said Charles had asked her to join him in Weymouth, and Darcy would explain the situation. The second note was of greater moment.

Dear Lizzie,
I add this to tell you we have decided to stay here for the night. Darcy must now have told you of the existence of the little girl – Charles' daughter – born shortly after he returned to Netherfield and did me the honour of asking for my hand. Imagine how impossible it was for him to tell me then. Last week he explained all the circumstances, hoping I might be willing to visit the child (but not the mother) during our stay in Lyme. Now an entirely new situation has arisen: the manager of a Canadian theatrical company wishes to marry the young woman - providing she gives up her baby. Imagine our distress. What will be the best thing for poor little Penelope? Her nursemaid is too young to be left in sole charge. Not that the mother means to desert her child immediately, but obviously she wants Charles to find a solution while he is in the area.

The carriage comes back without me and we shall travel together in the curricle tomorrow. (Yes I did take clothes with me, already knowing that Charles might be delayed overnight.) I grieve for him in this painful situation, but he approves me sharing all this with you, knowing your loving support will be a great comfort to me.

Kiss my darling little Edward. I fear this surprisingly hot weather may add to all the discomforts of teething.

In haste, your loving sister,
Jane

Elizabeth was so confused by this new development she re-read the letter several times to be certain she understood it. Even then her thoughts took her no further than fruitless wondering how everything could be managed for the general good. Jane appeared entirely concerned with the child, her generosity of spirit leaving no room for jealousy - unless she concealed it from herself?

Such a suspicion was bound to occur to Elizabeth, painfully reminded of her own rage and misery when first understanding that the woman she regarded as a friend was Darcy's ex-mistress. Nor was she entirely free of these feelings even now, despite the fact that the relationship belonged to the period when she actively disliked him, and he was struggling to deny his increasing regard for her. The same was not true of Bingley; only weeks before he took up with this actress the whole of Meryton had expected him to marry Jane. Her mother spoke of it triumphantly everywhere, but in fact he went up to London before any declaration had been made, and his continuing absence caused everyone's expectations (even Mrs Bennet's, her voice even louder in disappointment) to fade.

Jane, entirely good and honest herself, would have been no better prepared than the most ignorant child-bride to learn that Charles became a father at almost the moment he became her husband. Such successful duplicity in a man who had seemed so openly transparent was a painful reminder how little women understood the lives of men. All Jane's undoubted courage must have been called into action, and Elizabeth's first inclination - to voice her anger at Charles' feckless behaviour compounded by such polished deception - would only add to her sister's pain. If Darcy would consider having his past mentioned, might it help Jane to know that other respectable men had mistresses before they had wives?

Vainly struggling with confusion, Elizabeth greeted her husband's entrance with a smile of relief. She made room for him beside her so they could study the letter together, but apart from agreeing this was a complicated situation, he chose to continue with a general comment which expanded Elizabeth's unspoken feelings.

"Such a vast gulf exists between the young men and women of our class I am amazed we ever bridge it. Total innocence, extending in some cases to blinkered ignorance, is expected of our sisters and daughters, while for brothers and sons, amorous encounters before marriage are encouraged and adultery after marriage only too often condoned. That is where the real immorality lies and I can vouch that Charles Bingley finds it as repugnant as I do. The former has the ugliness of hypocrisy, but otherwise, as I think you now understand, even if you cannot approve, I consider such behaviour generally appropriate, and certainly the best way to avoid hasty, ill-considered, marriages. You know the rules I set for myself; Bingley made a more dangerous choice with the sadly familiar result of an unwanted child."

Her initial disgust with Charles somewhat lessened by her husband's words, Elizabeth's unspoken thoughts followed a lighter vein; if only Charles had consulted Darcy on this as on all other subjects, he would have been introduced to ladies too old (or too wise?) to make him a father.

Understandably, she confined herself to saying, "When you first spoke to me on this subject, I found my thoughts constantly reverting to it - being rather more surprised than I allowed myself to acknowledge."

"You looked surprised, but seemed attentive rather than shocked. And here is an irrational element; despite making a plea for greater openness, I would not want a young woman to be at ease with that aspect of the masculine world. My ideal is that such facts should be known in general rather than in particular, and only discussed between parents and children (of a suitable age) or men and women when they are as close to marriage as we were."

His wife offered her own reflections.

"It is true that most young women know more about tales of lurid abduction - from cheap novels or scandal sheets for example - than of the bachelor lives of the men in their own society, but notwithstanding your distaste for hypocrisy you have already agreed that the alternative is difficult to achieve. Of course a perceptive mind will gather some sense of probabilities, and with my usual vanity I believed myself in possession of such a mind, while making a crass misjudgement concerning Bingley at which I should either laugh or cry. How could I have been such a simpleton as to imagine, as I did, that a rich, handsome, amiable young man would avoid these adventures?"

"By choosing not to devote much thought to it. We all have predilections which we protect by avoiding general discussion, but one valuable exception should be conversations between man and wife."

Elizabeth's warm assent to that thought was diminished by her husband's next words.

"Although not in the same category of importance, there is something to discuss now. I beg you to be more aware of the effect weather has upon you."

"Weather?" she enquired doubtfully. "Admittedly thunder upsets me, but there has been none today."

"Thunder was in the air; that heavy stillness should have alerted you, and the rainstorm while you slept was accompanied by sheet lightening. I have only had the pleasure of living with you for eighteen months, but in some particulars I may know you better than you know yourself. Several times I have observed (Derbyshire offering such dramatic changes in weather) that the build-up before a storm affects you as much as the storm itself, with the influence being perhaps greater because you discount it. It makes you impulsive rather than rational, but let me hasten to say I measure this by your usually excellent disposition."

His final words were a relief to Elizabeth who believed too much was being made of exhaustion, which she considered only partially caused by following sea-bathing with an unexpectedly steep climb. While grateful for her husband's tender attentions she wished to defend the morning's exertions as quite within her powers, had it not happened that reasonable fatigue was exacerbated by anxiety about Jane and the hostile behaviour of Mrs Fitzwilliam. Almost certainly his reaction to this excursion (which she had hoped to enjoy in his company) was connected with his fixed dislike of her solitary walks, to her mind as irrational as those aspects of *her* behaviour now subject to criticism.

Feeling righteously forbearing, she intended a mild suggestion that perhaps it was enough for one day to be criticised by a stranger, when an alarming thought struck her. Could there be a faint similarity between the last few hours and scenes only too familiar at Longbourn – her mother's hysterical collapse when confronted by any real or imagined family trouble, followed by a retreat to her dressing-room attended by her maid and any of her daughters she could gather round her? There had had always seemed ample reason for Elizabeth to feel superior to Mrs Bennet's ignorance and emotional instability, but could some trace of the latter quality lurk in her own nature?

She listened anxiously, but her husband was affectionately entreating her to be on guard against allowing natural liveliness to lead to over-exertion. Before she could fully enjoy this unsolicited assurance that her actions in no way resembled her mother's, a baby's cry close at hand distracted them both. Darcy answered her unspoken question.

"The attics are unsuitable at midday in this unusual heat. Hearing Edward wailing miserably, I acted as your deputy by visiting the nurseries before coming to you. Until the temperature modifies I decided they should use rooms down here during the day, returning upstairs at bedtime. Poor Edward has an inflamed cheek and keeps rubbing at his ear to get rid of the discomfort; a hot room can only add to the problem. You must inspect the arrangements and see what you think of them. If the garden is cool enough now we could certainly extend the time the children spend there."

Every vestige of Elizabeth's irritation vanished.

"How truly thoughtful you are for us all; the best husband, brother, father."

The ideal husband responded dryly.

"Ensuring that my over-tired wife eats and rests, and that my over-heated daughter and nephew move to cooler rooms scarcely warrants this eulogy." Then with genuine feeling, "You cannot doubt that the central purpose of my life is to care for my family, to protect them and promote their happiness."

Painfully aware of the contrast between his loving concern and the general indifference displayed by her father, she replied affectionately, "You may scold me whenever you like."

"But I do not like, apart from the unworthy reason that it shows my adored wife has a few small faults to set against my much graver ones."

She and Darcy then entered upon those mutual reassurances so dear to a young couple.

"Possibly producing a certain complacence, but very strengthening to a marriage," concluded Elizabeth, with a smile so alluring that her husband felt they had better attend to the practicalities of daily life.

"If you feel rested enough, after your visit to the children we could walk through the garden to the upper path that overlooks the Cobb and the fishing boats."

"And go down to the Cobb itself? I have not yet walked its length."

"Tomorrow will be time enough; perhaps a walk for you and Jane, while Bingley and I go further afield, for some of our conversations will be best conducted in pairs."

"Dear Jane! I have no advice to offer, only my wholehearted support. How intensely she will suffer from knowing that beloved Edward is not her husband's first child. But that will never be admitted to me or anyone."

"I fear you are right; but your concern will be a vital comfort, even if there are pains she will not discuss and few possible suggestions to be made."

Darcy, however, had suggestions - even solutions - to offer his friend, and was confident his advice would be heeded. But it was scarcely appropriate for Jane to be involved, and out of the question for Elizabeth.

The Bingleys returned for breakfast next day, and exactly as Darcy had foretold the men set off together while the women sat in the garden near the children and their nurse maids.

"I am sorry I could not confide in you sooner, Lizzie. Charles assumed the satisfactory arrangements already in existence would continue, and merely wanted me to see the child and approve everything. But now the upheaval is alarming, though not yet felt by poor little Penelope. We decided, after all, that I should meet the mother. Her personality is as striking as her looks; there is so much life about her, and the baby is the same - greatly advanced for her age; talking, walking, very confident and full of quaint humour."

There being little more to report, the sisters rather ineffectually discussed possible arrangements. When Jane suggested moving the child closer to Dufton, Elizabeth pointed out the difficulties of an unacknowledged half-sister as a near neighbour to the legitimate children. Her own ideas shifted to the child living near Pemberley somewhat under her supervision, but they quickly realised the difficulties would be almost as great. Then Jane wisely decided they must delay further discussion until their husbands rejoined them, and by turning their attention to the charms of their own children the time passed happily until the men appeared and Charles burst into speech.

"Darcy and I have possibly found the ideal solution. In a few days we all to go to Tollington, and Mrs Fitzwilliam, the most capable person imaginable, can be consulted. Apparently she loves to organise, so possibly the child and her nurse could be settled in their village under the eye of Mrs Fitzwilliam who would keep us informed."

Turning to his wife he added, "We could come to this neighbourhood every summer, and therefore see Penelope, but not as an intimate, not in a way that would threaten our children, my dear."

Elizabeth stared at Bingley, speaking so cheerfully while his wife sat in shocked silence at the thought of strangers being made privy to all this. Darcy intervened quietly.

"Penelope can properly be described as a child deserted by her mother and therefore in need of protection; there is nothing untoward in this. As my cousin's new wife is active on behalf of the widows and children of soldiers, she might be of great assistance."

Jane objected to deception, but her husband tried to reassure her by arguing the likelihood of the Fitzwilliams deducing some closer tie, but not enquiring into details; such things were usually managed like this. He was so obviously ill at ease with a speech contrary to his open nature that, sensing his real anxiety, Jane murmured assent.

Had Elizabeth's views been called for they could only have caused confusion. With displeasure she imagined Mrs Fitzwilliam taking over the whole enterprise, paying little heed to the Bingleys and none at all to the Darcys, but a moment's thought made her reconsider; this was a woman equipped to offer practical solutions and the fact that she was unreasonably combative was irrelevant. Increasing intimacy with the wife of a man who was not only a cousin but also Darcy's lifelong friend, was unavoidable, so in her next conversation with Jane she felt impelled to soften her previous description of meeting Mrs Fitzwilliam. Her sister smiled.

"Lizzy, of course I recognised that some details were heightened; you excel in telling anecdotes against yourself; think of that first meeting with Darcy and your delight in quoting his comment describing you as tolerable, but not handsome enough to tempt him!"

"I refuse to see any similarity," said Elizabeth, defiantly, "despite the fact that both times I was reporting the words I heard."

"On the first occasion the speaker was noticeably out of humour, so the same may be true of the second, perhaps with the further excuse that Mrs Fitzwilliam was brusque from nervousness. The hostility of her husband's family has given her much to contend with."

"You shall not persuade me to be more tolerant of her manners than of Darcy's on that first occasion. I now have wide experience of my husband's magnanimous spirit and while Mrs Fitzwilliam may possibly be his equal, she has yet to prove it to me."

Although aware that her sister was still half-joking, Jane anxiously denied finding any fault in her brother-in-law, so Elizabeth chose that moment to describe something of Darcy's bachelor life to show that Bingley's amorous involvement was not unusual. Initially Jane was shocked rather than reassured; despite knowing of other entanglements (Wickham flashed into her mind) it had in no way prepared her to associate improprieties with these seemingly peerless husbands. It was some time before she was reluctantly persuaded that even honourable gentlemen were allowed such licence in the fashionable world, and given these standards both men had acted honourably. At the end of long cogitation her unspoken conclusion came surprisingly close to Elizabeth's impatient and facetious thought: she did momentarily wonder - given this new insight into masculine lives - if Charles would have fared better had Darcy introduced him to some of those amoral older women in High Society, thus reducing the possibility of a tragically unwanted child.

The hot weather abated, and despite their inescapable anxieties they all enjoyed the following days in Lyme, especially a windblown walk on the Cobb and a boat trip out of the harbour providing them with a view of the wide arching red-brown cliffs.

Edward was soon restored to his usual good humour, and late each afternoon the children were brought out to join their parents in the garden.

The Darcys needed only Georgiana to complete this harmonious family group, and she would arrive for a short visit the following week. Her letters were obviously concerned with the social life of various resorts, but she also devoted just as much space to describing the progress of the school at Pemberley. Miss Biggs had again invoked the help of the Porters; this time Maria - with the advantage of two years more seniority than Bella – had come to advise her. If the curate of Pemberley was ever going to declare an interest in her, surely this must be the time, thought Elizabeth.

No such thought crossed her husband's mind. His main concern was that Georgiana had not mentioned Lord James Scott, who apparently had been following her from one watering place to another and was always prominent among her party. He was one of the numerous sons of a Duke of vast wealth and several ancient titles, whose own life had been disreputable. It was greatly to the credit of this fifth son that he lived a quietly hardworking life managing one of the Duke's smaller estates in England, which would presumably be his patrimony. While determined not to infringe his sister's privacy, Darcy hoped she might choose to speak of him.

But before Georgiana's arrival, the visit to Tollington was to take place, and the four of them debated how to introduce the problem of Penelope to Mrs Fitzwilliam. They concluded - cumbersome though it seemed - that Darcy and Bingley would first speak to the Colonel who could then discuss it with his wife.

ཚ Scene Ten ཚ

*T*he cooler weather continued for their journey to Tollington Court; the first miles through dramatic coastal scenery, which was then replaced by gentler contours and increasingly isolated villages. As they had been forewarned, everything about the Court was in need of repair, but the shabbiness was not unpleasing, and it seemed to Elizabeth that Mrs Fitzwilliam proved more gracious as a hostess than a guest. The whole party walked together on the terrace overlooking the neglected parterre before the men climbed down to where piles of earth were being excavated for a water-garden.

"This is a project dear to the Colonel's heart," said his wife, "for campaign summers in the Peninsula made him long for all things watery, cool and green. The gentlemen are talking earnestly — particularly your husband, Mrs Bingley; perhaps he has first-hand experience? We are beginners, but have secured a man whose work is highly regarded - I hope your husband visualises the fountains, pools and cascades that will emerge from this wasteland of mud."

As Jane imagined that the question of little Penelope was even now being presented to the Colonel, she made a slightly incoherent reply before urging their hostess to describe the alterations and improvements. Relying on her increasing familiarity with the workshops at Pemberley, Elizabeth hoped to understand the discourse which followed, but such complicated details of measurements, materials and costs were instantly produced that the two listeners - who had never advanced beyond simple arithmetic, and whose minds were concentrated upon the future of one child rather than a large estate - had to call on all their powers of courteous attention.

Mrs Fitzwilliam, well satisfied with the accuracy of her report, then continued their walk, talking mainly to Jane, of whose life she knew little and whose beauty posed no threat to her husband's affections.

Elizabeth strolled beside them, perversely enjoying the crumbling beauties of the house and grounds in contrast to the meticulous condition of the Pemberley estate. She no longer felt guilty that, just occasionally, the splendours of her own home struck her as oppressive rather than pleasurable. There were even moments when she felt nostalgic for the casual life of Longbourn, until she remembered the noisy triviality of family conversation and her mother's relentless interference in her adult daughters' lives.

Lectures from Mrs Fitzwilliam must be regarded as preferable. Listening to her vigorous tones Elizabeth was convinced that Tollington would soon be ordered according to her wishes; did this apply to the Colonel as well? Courteous and attentive as ever, he yet seemed diminished in his wife's company, but if his health were restored, would the lively manners of Rosings return, or would her domination continue?

Their hostess was certainly a woman who acted decisively, for Jane came to her sister's dressing room before dinner to report that Mrs Fitzwilliam had already recommended the local village, with facts (in addition to her own presence) which would make it a highly suitable place for a little girl. Elizabeth having dismissed her maid in order to talk privately, Jane took over the task of arranging her hair, while Darcy looked appreciatively at two views of the young women — their real presence and their mirrored reflection. But it was his wife who commented when Jane left the room.

"Despite her anxieties, how well she is looking; that elaborate hairstyle, which would never suit me, enhances her natural beauty. Really she is incomparable."

Without apparent dissent, Darcy solemnly enquired, "As the sister of an incomparable beauty I assume the height of your ambition is to achieve a satisfactory appearance?"

In no doubt of his regard, Elizabeth laughed.

"The real task is to order my thoughts in a satisfactory fashion. Although it appears to go against her inclination as much as my own, I am determined to like Mrs Fitzwilliam. She is not an easy companion, though understandably more at ease with Jane than with me, but being so actively clever makes her infinitely superior to most of the people I know in Meryton, or even around Pemberley. So I agree to being improved by her information even if she addresses me as a public meeting rather than a person."

"Of the two of us," replied Darcy, "I am probably more averse to the marriage, yet believe you are wise to persevere with the acquaintance, which I judge to be even more to her advantage than to yours."

Choosing to ignore his wife's dubious expression, he continued, "While too dominated by her own thoughts and feelings to be sensitive of her audience, she is always well-informed and from your example may learn the advantages of listening as well as lecturing. And speaking of feelings, there is no doubt of her devotion to her husband, which I am sure must commend her to you almost as much as to me."

On this note of mutual agreement they entered the saloon, ready to enjoy the evening. Their host, turning from his companion to greet them, disclosed to their startled gaze the newly married Mrs Tollington, who had the advantage of being better prepared for the encounter. Darcy was given only a moment to offer felicitations to the former Mrs Cartwright before their hostess took him away to meet the General, while his wife, no such rescue in sight, struggled to get her feelings under control, an endeavour helped by the fact that Mrs Tollington was still speaking – although Elizabeth was oblivious to the actual words. As it was essential to her pride not to appear agitated she managed to steady her nerves enough to catch the final sentences.

"The pain of saying farewell to my son made me wish to return here rather than continue the wedding journey we had planned. It pleased my husband that I already consider the Dower House as our home in which we can be quietly together and close to dear friends."

Elizabeth answered with a few confused phrases, and Mrs Tollington (concealing her surprise at the awkward manners of the usually responsive Mrs Darcy) good naturedly continued to speak quietly of their mutual friends, the Fitzwilliams, until her listener was ready with appropriate questions about young Cartwright's travel plans.

Half-listening to the reply, Elizabeth resentfully acknowledged that Mrs Tollington's charm was not diminished by an unusually subdued manner – presumably caused by maternal farewells, which apparently dominated her feelings rather than wedding celebrations. When the General joined his wife she had time to observe them together; certainly he was extremely attentive and she invariably gracious, but no serious conclusion could be drawn from common politeness. Inevitably, a share of compliments was offered to Elizabeth, doing more credit to the General's goodwill than his command of language.

As Elizabeth and Mrs Tollington sat on either side of their host at dinner, there she experienced not only Colonel Fitzwilliam's knowledgeable and varied talk, but was forced to concede that when all three of them were involved the conversation became so lively that she was haunted by the shadow of her old admiration for Mrs Tollington.

Greater difficulties were to be expected when the ladies withdrew. There would be only four of them, with a hostess lacking the social skills to smooth over any awkwardness. Belatedly, Elizabeth realised there was no awkwardness for the ex-Mrs Cartwright who remained unaware that the rapport between herself and Mrs Darcy was at an end. On her side Elizabeth intended to replace it with a cool civility, which she relied upon being quickly adopted by that discerning woman. In anticipation the difficulties seemed insuperable, but in the event everything went smoothly, for Mrs Tollington guided the conversation into channels skilfully including all four of them.

During a pause, Elizabeth, as much provoked as pleased by this skill, moved to a window, ostensibly to enjoy the view, but actually to soothe her feelings by adopting an ironic attitude. Brides, she decided, were proving uncomfortable people to meet – though the difficulty had never been apparent before encountering these two women. Her abrasive relationship with the newly married Mrs Fitzwilliam appeared to have modified, but with Mrs Tollington the experience was infinitely worse, for she was confronted by a woman once admired, now heartily disliked.

If Elizabeth hoped to control her discomfort by identifying whims and inconsistencies in both ladies, she succeeded only with Mrs Fitzwilliam, whose behaviour certainly included oddities that could, hereafter, be dismissed with a smile. But the only fault in Mrs Tollington was mendacity; there was nothing even faintly laughable about that.

With such a discouraging conclusion, it was a relief that Mrs Fitzwilliam was the woman now approaching her.

"You know the Earl and Countess of Otterburn, I imagine?"

"Yes I do, and am grieved that the Countess, a woman I had learned to esteem, has separated herself from such an admirable son."

"For the sake of my fortune she might have overlooked my family if we had not been so highly visible in trade in Otterburn. At a young age I was helping my father in the drapery shop he managed on behalf of my grandfather, and soon grew better at measuring, reckoning and ordering than my parents. The Countess, approving of my abilities, showed me particular kindnesses - more than I received from my parents, who exploited my mental talents while despising my plain looks. My grandfather so entirely disagreed with their behaviour that he left them only a competence while the bulk of his fortune (vastly increased by supplying the Army) came to me. Now her Ladyship feels betrayed by me and I feel betrayed by her. There will never be a reconciliation."

The last words were spoken with a finality Elizabeth wished to dispute but feared was correct. With a sardonic look, suggesting she understood this confusion, Mrs Fitzwilliam concluded with, "I am concerned for my husband rather than myself, but we mean to be happy here, and the size of my fortune softens painful thoughts," then breaking off suddenly, "here are the gentlemen."

Clearly Mrs Fitzwilliam had already said more than she intended, for she turned away abruptly, paying her guest no further attention. This lack was corrected by the Colonel who begged Elizabeth for some music, then sat beside her turning the pages and reminding her of similar occasions at Rosings. Even with the presence of the Tollingtons the evening was agreeable enough to distract her thoughts from the problems of Charles' love child; she hoped Jane had enjoyed the same respite.

Next morning an early start was made for the village, where Elizabeth was surprised to see a number of the substantial cottages standing empty.

"When sheep farming flourished here," explained their hostess, "the large upper rooms originally contained a loom until this activity moved to the River Exe, where all the preparations that transformed wool into cloth became concentrated. I plan to house Army widows and children, giving them a chance to help themselves by their own exertions. Most importantly, at least two women must be capable of turning those large upstairs rooms into schoolrooms."

With a reassuring look at the Bingleys, she added, "I am already involved with several widows of junior officers, many of them pathetically young. Clinging to their shreds of gentility they may be overly conscious of the military hierarchy, so a mixture of other people would be useful. I have no doubt of receiving further applications, mainly by word of mouth."

Charles pronounced the scheme entirely admirable, while Jane, mildly but steadily, urged the peculiar needs of their ward; the nursemaid must be supervised, and any arrangement subjected to an unhurried trial period. As their hostess agreed at great length, both Darcys restricted themselves to a few words and supportive looks, although *he* foresaw a variety of problems and *she* visualised the awkward situation of a motherless little girl in a community formed of mothers and children. Mrs Fitzwilliam and the Bingleys then walked ahead, but Charles soon turned back to make their deliberations known to the other three.

"It is still early, and our kind friend suggests we make an excursion to Weymouth after breakfast; the distance is less than ten miles; I know Lizzie wishes to see the town, and we could call upon the little family."

Doubt was visible on all faces, but Elizabeth smiled involuntarily, recalling a remark made by Bingley soon after they first met - that whatever he did was done in a hurry. Her smile was taken for an approval she was far from feeling. Six people to make an unannounced visit to a 'little family', including a mother whose presence had not been acknowledged to the Fitzwilliams? Why had Jane not been able to prevent such imprudence?

Fortunately this was not the real situation. The nursemaid, taking Penelope with her, had returned to her own family for a time, where a visit from the Bingleys was half-expected. Elizabeth experienced an even greater surprise when Mrs Fitzwilliam insisted that the child and her attendant should occupy the nurseries at Tollington Court until suitable lodging was found. Jane looked anxiously at the Colonel, but quickly dismissing her fears he maintained it would be a pleasure to have a little girl about the place.

As soon as she was alone with her husband, Elizabeth exclaimed, "Never have I encountered such a woman; presented with complex problems she solves them within a few hours. Yet somehow I would not wish my concerns to come under her scrutiny, and I hope Jane will not find herself swept away on this tide of energy. So far everything seems to have fallen out well; Charles obviously thinks so."

Darcy added further reassurance. "Even though her voice may not be immediately heard, your sister will always resist anything she believes to be wrong. These proposals appear sound and include the advantage of a quick solution."

Elizabeth seized upon the final words.

"The speed greatly appeals to me; I am sick of all these half-truths and prevarications so contrary to Jane's truthful spirit. To my mind Charles has much to answer for. I suspect him of enjoying the frisson of excitement involved in all these stratagems."

"You misunderstand Bingley. Just as your sister, regardless of her feelings, is uniformly agreeable, so it is his nature to appear hopeful and ebullient whatever unhappiness lurks below the surface."

Darcy paused before continuing, "If you feel a new reserve between yourself and Jane it is because marriage changes circumstances; you are no longer the Miss Bennets living together and discussing everything together."

"No indeed not. But how lucky I am in the people I care for most; so different from each other, but alike in integrity. If I have not gained from such examples I must be beyond redemption."

"In that regard I have taught you nothing, and I imagine you contributed as much to your sister's moral education as she did to yours; possibly more, due to the quickness of your mind."

"Take care! You know how this appeals to my vanity; so before I become too complacent let me confess that personal resentment has a part in these proceedings. Mrs Fitzwilliam offers practical help beyond my powers, depriving me of a role I covet now that Jane is no longer free to share all her concerns with me." With an affectionate look, but a teasing note in her voice, she added, "Fortunately you have gone a long way towards making me accept your more sympathetic explanation of Charles' behaviour, and doubtless I will soon be fully persuaded. Reason has already prevailed in another direction. Although I pretended to joke about making a close friend of our new cousin, I was conceited enough to think she had some need of me. Now I see that her energies and talents are equal to anything, I shall be more comfortable observing her undoubted virtues from a respectful distance."

Elizabeth silently pondered whether or not this woman had also supplanted Darcy as Bingley's advisor. If it was so, her husband was not inclined to comment before they rejoined their party. Jane, naturally anxious for fresh topics of conversation, displayed her lack of guile by choosing Mrs Tollington as her subject.

"I understand why she is a favourite of yours, Lizzy. For true elegance of mind and address I have rarely met her equal. Now that her son is to be away, possibly for years, it is fortunate she has gained the comfort and companionship of a husband. During the years of her widowhood she must have had many admirers, but I suppose until recently she put her boy before everyone. Was there a friendship between him and Georgiana — or have I been mistaken?"

"You are entirely correct in calling it a friendship. In addition to the musical tastes they share, Georgiana (among other friends) also benefited from his familiarity with private art collections around London. A happy combination of youthful enthusiasm and expert knowledge made him the ideal tutor, but I discerned no romantic inclination on either side. Do you remember one particular contact you had with him?

Young Cartwright included us in an invitation to view English watercolours at Mr Fawkes'London residence (which happened to appeal more to my taste than to yours). He helped me select that Turner 'Landscape with Ruins', my first present to Darcy."

Her sister, scarcely recalling the landscapes so memorable to Elizabeth, made an apologetic reply. "You have done more than I have, Lizzie, to educate yourself about a variety of modern paintings. Charles and I are still trying to learn about modern oil portraits, rather than watercolour views. However, I would like to know where Darcy chose to hang his present?"

"Obviously it would not look well on Chinese wallpaper, so it hangs in our bedchamber where light from the east window falls on it. You must come and see it."

Jane showed an affectionate interest before her attention returned to the question previously occupying her thoughts.

"With one or two small exceptions your observations about people are usually trustworthy." Elizabeth, painfully aware of some egregious misjudgements, stifled an inclination to dispute this generous statement, and allowed her sister to continue.

"What do you think of General Tollington? A valiant soldier and undoubted gentleman, but do you think he can match his wife in breadth of culture?"

"In the briefest possible terms, no!"

"But of course that need not detract from other valuable qualities," said Jane, expanding on the general excellence of the newly married pair.

As she listened, Elizabeth struggled with her own thoughts. By keeping silent about Mrs Tollington I too have withdrawn from the open confidence I imagined we shared at Longbourn, but when I examine the past, restraints existed as soon as we grew up. There was Jane's desire that Bingley's departure from Netherfield not be further discussed, and my months of confused feelings about Darcy. The truth about Mrs

Tollington cannot be spoken, but this secret - and others inevitably developing in our lives - need not diminish our mutual trust.

She scolded herself into better sense, and consequently better humour. Mrs Fitzwilliam was solely motivated by altruism, and from now on her challenging manner would be considered acceptable rather than aggravating. She already felt less critical of Charles' appearance of ease, and now that Mrs Cartwright had become Mrs Tollington... Here Elizabeth stopped, refusing to include her in the amnesty. Only her absence would make her excusable.

Jane reclaimed her attention.

"Lizzie, I fear you have not been listening. Will you come with us to see Penelope? I hate to encroach on your time in Weymouth, but there will be other visits, and today I am anxious for your opinion. To decide without the benefit of your advice would be almost impossible for me."

Weymouth's splendours could not compete with Elizabeth's pleasure at this request, but the Colonel and Darcy had no intention of being uninvited visitors. The latter's steady concern for the child's welfare was entirely objective; he felt no curiosity about the individual and believed the group was already too large. His wife clearly wished to accompany Jane, otherwise he would have argued that her presence was unnecessary, even unbecoming. Fortunately he restrained himself, for the sisters, guided by their own good sense, decided that while the Bingleys called at the house to ask if Penelope might accompany them to the beach, the two additional ladies would wait at the waters edge.

The area was not yet fashionable, so the beach was occupied by fishermen, some of them helped by their elder boys and girls while younger children ran around in noisy play. Even as her companion instructed her about the advantages of growing up in the family trade, Elizabeth noticed a more prosperously attired pair – an active child running towards them while her attendant remained sitting on an upturned boat, raising her voice to summon the little girl.

"Miss Penny, come back here!"

Disregarding this instruction, Penelope (for there could be no doubt of her identity) ran confidently to them as to familiar friends. Jane's description of precocity still left them unprepared for the reality of so young a child speaking with amazing fluency as she generously offered each lady a shell, and pointed out with great satisfaction that one of them was wearing red boots like her own. The nursemaid's apologies could not disguise her pride in Miss Penelope, scarcely a year and a half, talking away like that: she had never heard her equal.

When she learned that Mr and Mrs Bingley were already at her parents' cottage, she proposed to take the child there at once. But Mrs Fitzwilliam and Penelope were so busy about red boots, and shells, and a pattern the former was drawing in the wet sand that the latter stopped talking only to draw breath for protesting screams which were not easily calmed. Relieved that the raising of this excitable prodigy was not to devolve on her, Elizabeth wondered how her companion felt today about the assistance so warmly proffered yesterday? The tumult of the following minutes made speech impossible and observation difficult, and while the sobbing child was being dragged away it chanced that Mrs Fitzwilliam was unusually brief and inaudible. However, the words 'a serious challenge' were sympathetically overheard.

Elizabeth's reasonable assumption was incorrect; far from being deterred Mrs Fitzwilliam had compelling reasons for being drawn to Penelope. She too had been a forward and excitable child, in her case severely disciplined by her family until that quickness made her useful in the shop at an early age. She had suffered under the further disadvantage of being plain, but Penelope showed promise of unusual beauty. Why should her lack of acknowledged family consign her to a modest marriage at best, lonely spinsterhood at worst? The scrupulous Bingleys would always provide a suitable allowance, but if it seemed appropriate the Fitzwilliams could enhance the child's natural gifts with wealth and social position.

This thought - which had arisen when first hearing the story - in no way interfered with Mrs Fitzwilliam's hopes of giving birth to her own child, despite being older than she looked. If the Colonel only visualised the little girl as a temporary member of their household, his wife was confident of changing his mind if she decided on this course of action. There was ample money to provide for several children, and having one already settled in their nursery would be a consolation if they were not blessed with a child of their own. Although her feelings were strong-willed and passionate, Mrs Fitzwilliam possessed a rational mind. Nothing was to be forced; a year, years, might pass before any of this was spoken of, but she could imagine no possible difficulty with Charles Bingley. (She naturally assumed his paternity.)

Unaware of the full extent to which they might be indebted to Mrs Fitzwilliam, the Bingleys, travelling back to Lyme Lodge with the Darcys, felt that the current arrangements were greatly to Penelope's benefit - especially as Betsy, the nursemaid, was to be joined by her younger sister.

They would be company for each other, and, as an extra advantage, schooling was to be arranged for

them by the indefatigably philanthropic Mistress of
Tollington Court.

❦

Scene Eleven

❦

The journey took four hours, time enough for the Darcys to put aside anxieties concerning Charles' natural daughter and the unwelcome reappearance of the former Mrs Cartwright, and concentrate their thoughts on the happiness of being with Cecilia and Georgiana again. No intractable situations were likely to arise with either of them; at worst Cecilia might suffer some minor indisposition or Georgiana be disinclined to talk about her friendship with James Scott.

The Bingleys were in a less enviable position; with their Tollington hosts shortly arriving for a visit, distance would bring only a few days relief from their problems. Penelope's future was of great interest to Mrs Fitzwilliam; her enthusiasms were strong, but among her virtues, delicacy of feeling was not noticeable. Neither of the mild natured Bingleys felt equal to the task of explaining their ardent wish to give all their attention to baby Edward, free of painful reminders of this other child.

On arriving home, Jane had the pleasure of finding her son awake and full of smiles, but Elizabeth had to be satisfied with the little that was visible of Cecilia peacefully asleep in a shadowed corner of the nursery. Left free to attend to other matters she was intrigued to learn that Lord James Scott had already left his card, though fully aware Georgiana was not expected until the following day. This was encouraging proof that he wished to meet her family. Charles, eager for new people and new activities, provided extra information.

"I realise that Caroline is at this moment the guest of Countess Strachan, one of this young man's sisters, but in that numerous family I believe there is little contact with her youngest brothers. As the Duke's eldest daughter she inherited that title and an estate which is an integral part of the ancestral lands."

"What an excellent idea," said Elizabeth, always responsive to the status of daughters.

"The Dukedom still goes to the eldest son."

"Never mind; I am no enemy to benefits being shared."

"Neither he nor his Duchess have been a good example to their children. In fact they lived apart for many years, leaving the youngest boys in the home of a cousin who prepared them for the relatively modest style of life that will be their lot. The family seems split down the middle; the elder siblings are much with their father, in particular the Countess who acts as his hostess."

"While the others support their mother's side of the quarrel?"

Darcy intervened.

"The difference made between elder and younger children in that family has an explanation that reflects no credit on either parent. For some years they lived in a *ménage a trois,* the Duke's mistress effectually supplanting the Duchess, with the natural children apparently being almost as dear to their father as the existing legitimate ones - and patently dearer than the legitimate ones born after the liaison ended.

"Perhaps it is not surprising that, after a period almost approaching respectability, it was the wife who began to stray. When questions were raised about the legitimacy of a child, born a few years after James Scott, the Duchess and her baby followed her lover abroad. They moved about a great deal, and in recent years ill health has kept her out of the public eye.

Her death a few months ago was presumably something of a relief to her estranged family; excusably enough the lady is spoken of no more in death than she had been in life, but less excusably, the husband continues his habit of rarely seeing his younger sons. Considering this family history James Scott must be admired for becoming an upright young man making a success of the estate it is presumed he will inherit."

Jane, wishing to advance some extenuating circumstances for a least one of the parents, preferably both, found the task impossible and remained silent. Elizabeth, though equally disgusted was not equally incredulous. She even experienced a momentary sense of triumph that in the less exalted society from which they sprang such situations would never be tolerated, until her quick mind admitted that those who lived out of the public eye could more easily conceal indiscretions. They both satisfied themselves with praising the moral character of the young man they were soon to meet.

"And in Scotland," added Charles, possibly feeling he should defend his sister's choice of friends, "the presence of the Countess has ensured that her father's household is above reproach. The days of his excesses seem to be over."

Inevitably this history increased Elizabeth's curiosity about Georgiana's potential suitor. Alas, during his first visit he was so little animated as to make decidedly dull company, and not even the good proportions of his figure and features (his height well above average) could give him a commanding appearance. This was in striking contrast to Darcy whose very air of reserve invariably drew eyes towards him. Elizabeth felt actively dismayed at the thought of Georgiana being matched with a partner equally inclined to silent gravity, but while admitting this as a possible difficulty her husband determined to come to no conclusions before hearing Georgiana's views.

She was careful to explain that this formal call had been unfavourable to Scott's powers of conversation, his speech being deliberate rather than quick. Then, leaving the subject of their visitor, she became infinitely more animated in speaking of Cecilia's engaging smiles, and of how greatly she looked forward to welcoming Colonel Fitzwilliam's bride. Yet even in the brief comment about James Scott there was some change in her manner, something less tentative, more self-assured.

Soon after his arrival, the Colonel offered Elizabeth an unexpected explanation for Georgiana's new air of confidence: Scott, notwithstanding his sedate appearance, had reawakened the ardent love she had once felt for a highly unsuitable man; feelings ill applied on that first occasion were now finding a more appropriate outlet.

It startled Elizabeth to realise that the Colonel, while too discreet to pronounce the name, had alluded to Wickham, knowing perfectly well that this scoundrel was now her brother-in-law. It was an undignified, almost farcical, circumstance, that not only had she and her sister Lydia been beguiled by him, but at an earlier date, Georgiana also. Even though her own short lived preference, causing little notice at the time, was now long forgotten, she answered cautiously, while conceding to herself that Georgiana might indeed share her brother's combination of passion and reserve while sadly lacking his invincible assurance.

Before long the Bingleys discovered they had no reason to worry about Mrs Fitzwilliam's discretion, for Penelope's name was only mentioned in a general conversation with Georgiana about a variety of social projects. The elder lady appeared at her best - informative but not domineering and surprisingly ready to wait for slowly articulated questions from a younger, less incisive, person.

During these discussions, when Miss Biggs, Maria Porter, and the Pemberley Schools, were mentioned, Elizabeth was curious enough to enquire about Mr Warriner, the person nominally in charge.

Georgiana looked at her brother.

"I believe you may be hearing from him soon. It is widely expected in the neighbourhood that he will resign his curacy to marry a lady of independent means, who lives about fifty miles away. With increasing frequency it has occurred to me that the engaging way in which he petitions young ladies for help might somewhat mislead them, but I soon learned that Maria Porter had already perceived this for herself. Now he will be free to devote all his time to Natural History which is clearly the major passion of his life."

This sharp criticism (by Georgiana's standards) effectively disposed of any romantic hopes entertained by Miss Porter or Miss Biggs. In a minor way Mr Warriner, appearing so guileless, was something of a philanderer, but it seemed to Elizabeth no bad thing that young women be exposed to a degree of gentle trifling as they made their way through the elaborate dances of courtship.

The second day of the Fitzwilliams' visit brought a letter from Caroline Bingley to her brother Charles, who now shared it with his wife and their hosts. Caroline had accepted an offer of marriage from her host, the Duke of H. - that wicked roué, as the household at Lyme universally considered him, and in any case a man with about twelve children, most of them older than Caroline. Charles was considerably baffled; it was all so contrary to his own amiably domestic habits, but in worldly terms an outstanding match, and he had long suspected that Caroline aspired to being a great figure in the world. Disappointed by Darcy her hopes had become more, not less, ambitious. Her brother tried to reassure himself with thoughts of the respectable daughter, Countess Strachan, but reading through a degree of circumlocution he gathered that Caroline was even now preparing to leave for their sister's house in London as the Countess found herself unable to approve of the engagement.

The Bingleys and the Darcys sat silently absorbing this news, but not surprisingly the latter pair were quick to move on to the next complication - the friendship between Georgiana and Lord James Scott. Within moments Elizabeth's ironic spirit envisaged Caroline Bingley not only as one of Britain's senior Duchesses, but the mother-in-law of Georgiana; with what delight would she play her role, particularly if condescending to visit Pemberley.

Darcy, who had hitherto reassured himself that James Scott had almost no contact with the unprincipled Duke, was dismayed to find that the Bingleys would now bring the connection closer, but, unlike his wife, was engaged in immediate practicalities rather than the more ludicrous details. If Charles had heard from his sister, surely James Scott must have heard from his father? It might also be expected that Charles, as Caroline's closest male relation, would receive a letter from her prospective husband? Then he reminded himself that the Duke, his status and wealth unassailable, had never considered himself bound by any social conventions.

In fact, the next communication received was a note to Bingley from young Scott, suggesting they meet at his lodgings to discuss the news, totally unforeseen by him, that their families were to be closely connected. Everyone present was impressed by the good sense of this arrangement, which included the additional advantage of convenient timing by allowing Charles to depart just before Georgiana and the Fitzwilliams assembled for breakfast. Darcy strove to present the betrothal as a routine piece of news, with Georgiana almost inaudibly following his lead, clearly grateful to her brother for not identifying her as possibly having a future connection with the Ducal family.

Conversation was unavoidably forced and uneven. Colonel Fitzwilliam, as joint guardian of Georgiana, wished to allude to James Scott in the context of the parental marriage, but felt obliged to be as discreet as Darcy whose concern was not only for Georgiana, but also for the Bingleys. The reserve imposed by her host was particularly welcome to Jane, whose admiration for Mrs Fitzwilliam stopped short of any wish to hear her pronounce judgement on the transgressions of sister Caroline's duke. It was tedious, albeit excusable, that the tradesman's daughter seized every opportunity to condemn scandals in High Society.

It was to be a busy morning for James Scott. Having (with stiff propriety) greeted Bingley as the brother of the lady who was shortly to become his mother, he returned with him to Lyme Lodge to petition for the hand of Miss Darcy. To all appearances untroubled by the slightly comic aspect of gaining, from two different sources within the space of one day, the promise of a wife in addition to a mother, the dullness and inflexibility of his manner became even more apparent.

Scott had hoped for an unobtrusive conversation with Mr Darcy, but this proved impossible, as Colonel Fitzwilliam, joint guardian, must also be summoned. The suitor regretted that everyone was thus alerted to the purpose of his visit, but although his own fortune was small he was confident of his eligibility. Admittedly it was a disquieting fact that his father's life was a disgrace, but the family titles were among the most ancient and richly endowed in the British Isles; the private life of the current holder could not diminish their power.

Initially, both Georgiana's guardians found themselves appreciating his inherent dignity, despite the wearisomely dull phrases about Miss Darcy encouraging his addresses and the alliance being beneficial to both families. He became more animated when claiming that the last few years showed a steady improvement in the Littlefields estate, despite his modest financial resources. At the conclusion of this stilted speech he urged an early marriage, as his bride's generous dowry would enable him to purchase an adjoining estate.

This last statement reversed Darcy's previous opinions. With all the considerable hauteur at his command, he announced that his sister's capital would be reserved for the benefit of herself and her children should any disaster overtake her husband. Quite unperturbed, Scott pointed out that the purchase of land would be of lasting advantage to his family; in all probability Miss Darcy would approve.

"The subject must not be raised with her."

"But I may ascertain the state of her feelings?"

If only he displayed more feeling himself, thought Darcy, angrily, as he allowed his cousin to answer for them both.

"That is certainly the next step to take, but she will naturally consult with us before giving you a final answer."

As soon as the young man left, Darcy burst out: "I no longer think he will do. It seems he has chosen

Georgiana as a suitable partner by birth and fortune, not least because her thirty thousand pounds will compensate for his mere twelve or fifteen thousand. I doubt that he has any real feeling for her."

"I must disagree with you, Darcy. He is not offensively cold-blooded. A tendency to be cautious, to plan carefully, is compatible with being a good husband and father. If Georgiana really wants this match, I would be inclined to argue the case for James Scott but ultimately leave the decision to you. Your affections and understanding must weigh more heavily than mine."

"I admit that he bears a remarkably good character in the world considering the difficulties under which he has laboured," conceded Darcy, "but it deeply offends me to have him already deciding how to use my sister's dowry. Nevertheless I am influenced by your argument, Henry, from the very fact that your cousinly concern for Georgiana, being less fervent than a brother's feelings, allows you to be impartial. Perhaps I am unreasonably biased, but I would certainly scorn a partner greedily anxious to get hold of my money."

"Your marriage already proves that," agreed his cousin affectionately, "but in my judgement young Scott genuinely means to promote their mutual welfare. You react too strongly, Darcy, having always been a liberal man yourself, as your father was before you. He passed on to you not only the inclination but also the means to indulge it. Think of Scott's parents, and his position as a neglected son poorly endowed considering his father's fabulous wealth."

With a nod, Darcy conceded the strength of his cousin's argument but broke off the conversation in order to seek Elizabeth's opinion. Her response wavered between his view and the Colonel's.

"I had already cautioned myself that merely because Scott's manner in society superficially resembles yours, it does not guarantee that he has all your good qualities."

Her husband was happy to accept this compliment, but honesty required him to add, "My cousin very properly reminded me that I had a father from whom to inherit good qualities, and who thereafter nurtured their growth and provided the income to act upon them. I am chastened to think how little is due to my own efforts."

"You would never have spoken in the crass way Lord James did today. Nor would your cousin, whose upbringing is a little closer to Scott's, due to the Otterburns placing the claims of primogeniture above all other. Yet despite faults in James Scott's character, if Georgiana does choose him after due consideration..?"

"My cousin and I would respect a decision made after time for reflection," said Darcy glumly. "I imagine she is half expecting his proposal and means to accept, subject to our approval."

Soon after this conversation, Georgiana sought them out to ask her brother's consent to her engagement, and received this reply.

"I would wish you to reflect for at least two months before giving a definite answer." This requirement was further expanded by, "I think Scott should visit Pemberley. To see him in your own home – the home of your family for centuries – will be more significant than meeting in the inevitably trivial social round of watering places. It would be wise to use this extra time to discuss your expectations of each other. For example, it occurs to me that his view of himself as head of the family (and every family must acknowledge a head) may be more inflexible than mine."

This must certainly frighten Georgiana, was Elizabeth's silent reflection. She has never allowed herself to query her brother's opinions and looks on me with alarm when I dare to do so. But perhaps she is learning to regard my behaviour as entirely proper for a wife?

As if to support this view, Georgiana looked questioningly at her sister. Uncertain what to say, Elizabeth settled for, "On slight acquaintance Lord James is so extremely reserved that I must leave you understand the degree of his affection and your response to it. Naturally I consider him wonderfully fortunate to gain your love, and can imagine your aims in life are compatible. If it is correct that he means to manage his estate without the assistance of a steward he will welcome your willingness to be involved in practical matters. For example, through the Miss Porters and Miss Biggs you have learned about the organisation of a school for children of estate workers; have you happened to discuss such things with him?"

As Georgiana was already feeling the tug of conflicting loyalties, her nervously vague reply meant the subject was discontinued just as Darcy's concern was aroused. Although generally urging this kind of involvement, he always assumed there would be a perceived difference between Miss Darcy and the Misses Biggs or Porter. He did not visualise Georgiana in daily supervision of estate children any more than being busy with the poultry yard or the training of unskilled maids. Presumably marriage to a member of one Britain's noble families, combined with her own substantial fortune, would continue to distance her from these tasks. While Darcy had inevitably noted Georgiana's ease with people whose restricted incomes dictated a modest style of life - the Gervase family at Kympton, Mr Warriner, even Miss Biggs - he viewed it as a temporary stage. It had not yet occurred to him that if Lord James Scott's mode of life fell somewhere between that of Farmer Biggs and

Fitzwilliam Darcy, his sister might be well content rather than merely resigned.

Leaving these silent conjectures, he asked for – and received - his sister's assurance that no final answer be given while the party remained at Lyme. This was in direct opposition to her suitor's wishes. Scott had hoped for an immediate agreement, shortly to be followed by his promised wife making an extended visit to Colonel Fitzwilliam at Tollington - so conveniently close to his own estate, Littlefields, to which he hoped to take his bride with the minimum of delay. For the short time they were alone together Georgiana had tentatively agreed with her lover, but this decision was nullified when her brother made his views known. In this confrontation of two unbending characters, she still deferred to her brother. Georgiana's reasons were purely personal, but worldly judgement would also have favoured Darcy, who had the habit of command natural to the master of Pemberley, whereas Scott (however confident his self-assessment) was merely to inherit a small property far from the glories of the princely estates owned by his father.

The young man was thoroughly displeased by Darcy's stipulations, but consoled himself with the thought that he would soon be the beneficiary of Georgiana's basically proper sense of duty, which would be transferred from the brother to the husband when Miss Darcy became Lady James Scott. If Georgiana was not yet ready to debate within herself the relative influence of an elder brother and a successful suitor, Scott felt no doubt that when married she would defer to the higher claims of a husband.

Elizabeth's delight in the Dorset coast had been only little interrupted by encounters with Mrs Fitzwilliam, with Bingley's illegitimate daughter, and with Darcy's ex-mistress, for at least all these people were living in the area she longed to explore. But Caroline Bingley's news brought to a sudden end her brother and sister's visit to Lyme Lodge. A second letter followed the first, this time requesting her brother's return to Dufton in order to provide her with an appropriate home in which to receive the Duke before their marriage. Although the tone of the letter was unattractively close to a demand, Charles was a solicitous brother, and Darcy, when consulted, agreed that the small London house of a mere brother-in-law was a less fitting address for the affianced bride of a great nobleman. He fully supported the Bingleys' wish to be on the road home within a few days.

Well acquainted with Jane's unselfish spirit, Elizabeth could only endorse the decision despite her own disappointment; Lyme would not be the same without her sister and family. But as it happened, the Darcys almost instantly found reasons to start their return journey. Now that James Scott was committed to visiting Pemberley it was necessary for him to curtail his holiday and return to supervising his own property for some weeks.

With the benefit of hindsight it seemed increasingly probable that all his holiday excursions had been planned around the pursuit of Georgiana Darcy. What she was too modest to think of for herself now occurred to her family as a likely scheme for a well-born young man who rarely came to London. But the speed with which mutual attraction developed was far beyond anything Scott might reasonably have expected – and a fact deeply regretted by Georgiana's brother.

To Darcy's mind only the tattered rags of the holiday remained, but he amused himself by planning a surprise for his wife. Express messages were sent to those who had been their hosts on the journey down, and it was agreed that on the return journey they would all be happy to entertain Georgiana and Mrs Annesley, who were to take charge of Cecilia and her nursemaids. Fortunately the two ladies warmly endorsed this plan (for had they felt otherwise they would certainly have disguised it) leaving everyone pleased with arrangements enabling Fitzwilliam and Elizabeth Darcy to extend their stay in Lyme before travelling home in a faster carriage.

They greatly enjoyed a few days alone together, free from the unexpected problems of Charles' daughter and the inevitable duties, welcome but demanding, which awaited them on their return to Pemberley. They celebrated their first day by exploring a great length of those enticing cliffs. Each additional mile was more dramatic and challenging than the original track climbed by Elizabeth in her first hurried venture, but to the blessing of cooler weather and suitable footwear was added another advantage organised by her husband; their carriage met them at the end of the walk.

Their last stop on the homeward journey was Kympton, where they were relieved to see Mrs Gervase almost recovered from her long illness, but alarmed to hear she was expecting a second child. Commonsense could only deplore this. While the joys of reunion, after weeks of anxious concern and enforced celibacy, awoke strong sympathies in Darcy, he hoped never to be guilty of exposing Elizabeth to the dangers of pregnancy if her health was in any way weakened - but then a clergyman presumably believed everything should be left to Divine Providence. Consequently he felt an exasperated mixture of sympathy and criticism for Gervase, particularly as the elder child was still frail and might remain so for some time.

Despite that anxiety, the family, with the marked exception of old Mrs Gervase, gave thanks for dangers past and were much in the mood to celebrate a happiness to come: Maria Porter was to marry Farmer Biggs. For the next few months it was her adamant determination to remain at Kympton helping her sister, a decision her lover could only approve, despite his impatience to be married.

Talking it over with her husband, Elizabeth rather facetiously wondered how the young man had been able to choose between two admirable young women. She might have fancied that the friendly smiles of the younger sister, Bella, would show to greater advantage. Perhaps in the end he decided that seniority must be allowed to count?

"Maria Porter need not rely on that claim," protested Darcy in support of his favourite: "Neither of them can be faulted in character, but I am convinced the elder one has the better mind."

"And you believe this is what Mr Biggs is seeking?"

Darcy wished he had chosen his words with greater care, for he did not associate a tenant farmer – however respectable and competent - with the quality of mind he attributed to Maria Porter. However, he had consistently maintained that Georgiana was unlikely to introduce those girls to possible husbands, whereas the circle in which Miss Biggs moved was much more suitable. Rationally he must stay with this opinion and assume that Biggs deserved his bride.

Elizabeth approved this attitude, adding, with a smile, "Your first assessment has been proved accurate so far. But while Miss Biggs can certainly spare a brother to one of her new friends, I rather doubt the environs of Pemberley will offer a wide selection of suitable young men, and perhaps she would like one for herself. At the tenants' Ball, Mr Biggs stood out as an educated and gentlemanly young man, but on all other occasions Mr Warriner seemed to have the field to himself and now he is to desert our local congregation for a rich widow. Perhaps we have a duty to put eligible bachelors in the Pemberley parsonage, moving them on as soon as they marry one of our local girls."

"You almost persuade me to place the whole thing in your hands, but, Elizabeth, you must bear in mind that although my inheritance involves several clerical livings, they do not all fall vacant exactly when required. You may find yourself involved in endless manoeuvres and permutations. Why not leave it all to the usual network of family and friends?"

Though this had not yet been a great success for the younger Bennet girls, Elizabeth was very ready to agree, adding, "And as far as Bella Porter is concerned we must give Mr and Mrs Gervase a chance."

This light-hearted conversation took place on their first day back at Pemberley, while they rode together through the hanging woods behind the house to the moors beyond. Looking down from the natural grandeur of rocky crags to the parkland below, both Darcys instinctively turned to each other with a joyful sense of being home. Lyme was not more lovely than this, and all importantly, they were not transient visitors but the careful stewards of the landscape. Darcy pointed out several groves of young trees planted by his father, one, in particular, extending up a steep hillside almost to the point where they stood.

"This, among the other projects, was planted soon after my mother's death. My father believed that schemes dedicated to future growth were her best memorial and generously involved me in every aspect. It is no wonder he was universally beloved at Pemberley, combining (as I, perhaps tediously, emphasise) a high sense of personal honour with a tolerant acceptance of other people's failings. While I hope he taught me the first quality, I could never achieve the second, but perhaps it proved a useful counter balance that I inherited my mother's less tolerant nature.

"My father treated me almost as an equal in family affairs when I was still a boy in years, particularly in everything concerning Georgiana. As she was only four when our mother died, this showed wisdom, not weakness, for as his own health deteriorated he was preparing me to take over the paternal role. And in that role, during the weeks following Georgiana's return to Pemberley I intend to exert my influence against James Scott whenever an opportunity presents itself. I am supported by the belief that my benevolent father would not have approved of this cold man any more than I do."

He then changed the subject.

"Now, my dear, let us discuss an easier problem. Taking this way home means a precipitous descent, but I would like to examine the trees in detail. If I lead, and you leave your mare to pick her own way, will you accept my assurance you have nothing to fear?"

Elizabeth, attracted by the route - one of the walks she had been instructed not to take alone - most willingly accepted his assurance and the following instructions.

"Slacken your reins and don't feel too proud to hold onto Elan's mane; with your lack of experience the situation poses some problems, but I shall watch over you."

There was no doubting this. Elizabeth gazed at his broad upright back and the glimpse of profile as his head moved from side to side assessing the trees before turning round in the saddle to see how she fared. Always so responsible, she thought fondly, was it any wonder the protective feelings for his little sister instilled in young Fitzwilliam Darcy never changed? I am too opinionated to succumb entirely to his management - and for the sake of our marriage and our children must remain so regardless of his greater knowledge in most areas - but Georgiana needs to get away.

Despite a wifely reluctance to entertain disloyal thoughts, the idea grew that James Scott, whatever his insensitivities, was the right man for Georgiana. She showed more confidence with him than she ever managed with Darcy, and it was part of life's natural progression that a brother's influence should be weakened by marriage and geographical distance.

Elizabeth felt increasingly convinced that this hard-working farmer of impeccable lineage offered exactly the right mixture; he would respect Georgiana's family background while appreciating the practical skills Georgiana obviously wished to develop. In this ideal picture there was no immediate place for music and books, but despite his retired life, Scott was no country bumpkin, and had made his choice after observing a highly educated young woman.

She wished her husband's character were not displayed to such advantage just now; it was a wretched business having to combine admiring love with the conviction that his dear sister needed to escape from him. Fortunately, speech between them was inadvisable, for the swaying rump and swishing tail of Darcy's horse made her mare hang back nervously, causing them both to concentrate upon getting her safely down the steep incline. She smiled, privately believing that she would have managed better on foot, criss-crossing in and out of the grove.

When they reached a level path enabling them to ride abreast, Darcy having given his decision against James Scott, chose not to speak of it again, merely asking his wife's views about varying the trees in the plantation. These were reassuring topics for Elizabeth, who had her own reasons for wanting to avoid further conversation about the projected marriage. Honesty would compel her to express her approval, and she feared her husband would identify this divergent opinion as criticism of the brotherly role he had fulfilled so tenderly.

Georgiana managed to resist her brother's influence, for soon after her suitor's arrival they presented themselves to Darcy and Elizabeth as a couple engaged and hoping for an early marriage. Both young people looked sedate rather than ecstatic, but Elizabeth, remembering that Darcy's grave public demeanour continued after he became an accepted lover, hoped his sister was enjoying an equal depth of happiness. This was not the moment to discuss money so James Scott caused no new offence, even winning an unexpected surge of approval by displaying a genuine love of music. His praise of Georgiana's performance later that day was warm and discriminating, causing her to colour with pleasure when he added that in their domestic evenings they might embark on duets despite his inferior talent and training.

In private she assured her brother and sister that she loved and respected Scott and was confident they were well suited to each other. Darcy was bound to accept these sentiments but wished he could feel more warmth for his new brother. It was no consolation that there were three of his wife's sisters for whom he cared even less, for this awkwardness was minimised by the fact that Elizabeth's own feelings for them amounted to no more than dutiful concern, unlike his devotion to Georgiana.

Having secured the hand of Georgiana Darcy, James Scott's anxiety to return to his work must give way to the

superior claims of a duty visit to his father, the guest of
the Bingleys at Dufton Hall. It might be imagined the
father's lack of interest would at least equal the son's,
but it happened that the Duke's characteristic
indifference to his younger children was stirred into
something approaching curiosity by the degree of
excited anticipation he sensed in his chosen bride. It
seemed more than was warranted by the mildly risible
circumstance that her friend Georgiana Darcy would
shortly become her daughter-in-law.

The Duke was a pleasure-loving man, whose
urbane manners thinly disguised complete selfishness.
Used to surrounding himself with people anxious to
amuse him, advancing years now inclined the Duke
towards a quieter life - a preference complicated by the
longstanding habit of depending on others for his
entertainment. The Bingleys were agreeable enough, but
far from exciting; worse than that, his son was known to
be a taciturn prig and in all likelihood Darcy would
prove to be a similar type. Identifying the cause of
Caroline's excitement might liven the amiably dull party
at Dufton until the arrival of more stimulating friends of
his own.

To her family, Georgiana's engagement had
been viewed as a solemn commitment rather than a
celebration; by contrast the atmosphere at Dufton
appeared almost frivolous, even on the first evening
before the Duke's guests arrived. Caroline Bingley's
clothes and jewels set off the victorious sparkle in her
eyes, despite an endeavour to appear becomingly modest
as she hung on the arm of her Duke while they received
the appropriate congratulations.

There was nothing much about him, was
Elizabeth's first impression - apart from his title and the
fact he carried his age well considering the life he led.
Within minutes this view was amended; a man of noble

lineage, intelligent and not positively ill looking, will never be insignificant, and geniality combined with high rank has its attractions. She began to find his company pleasant until witnessing the superficial affability with which he greeted a son he had neglected to see for several years. James Scott's coldly respectful words to his father must be preferred to such insincerity.

Then Caroline Bingley greeted her dear friend Georgiana Darcy, affecting embarrassment at the quaint fact that they were to become mother and daughter, but secretly delighted that she had captured a Duke while the Darcy heiress had accepted a fifth - or was it sixth - son almost totally disregarded by his father.

The Bingleys, hosts of this interesting party, allowed Caroline to adopt a proprietary attitude implying that Dufton had long been her home. This must be reckoned no small achievement with an estate so recently acquired, but it was her moment of triumph and under her management everyone was to be joyful. If she did not entirely succeed with the Darcys, there was compensation when the other chosen guests arrived with their effusive praise and congratulations.

A more moderate reaction was shown by the Bingleys' neighbours, the Jeffersons – a family already known to the Darcys. There were noticeable similarities between Bingley and Mr Jefferson in situation, general tastes, and attitudes; but the latter, having inherited Wychwood from his father a decade ago, was in a position to offer useful advice about managing an estate of comparable size in this particular part of the country. As he was already instructing his younger brother (a Naval Captain whose serious wounds made further active service impossible) it was a matter of course that Charles Bingley was invited to join them at any time. Thus a special warmth and intimacy had developed between the two families.

Among the people assembled there was enough variety for most people to find something to enjoy, and – knowing the visit would be brief - the Duke found himself willing to forego witty gossip for the unpretentious, yet respectful, attention that surrounded him, most particularly in the person of that beautiful Mrs Bingley. For their part, the Bingleys, expecting to meet a raddled old man, were relieved to find this notorious rake looking, and behaving, so well. At that moment they felt that wealth and status were not, after all, his only attractions.

The good humour was unfeigned. Scott's father, always astute in matters of business, showed his approval of Miss Darcy's munificent dowry by seeking out her brother to support his son's plan to use some of it to repurchase lost acres. He repeated facts already known to Darcy: by a regrettable error of judgement the farm had been sold off in the last generation; it was prime agricultural land which clearly rounded-off the estate.

Georgiana's brother, restating his determination that her dowry should not provide the purchase money, waited silently for further speech - to the surprise of the nobleman who had automatically assumed their business discussions would be prefaced by Darcy's compliments about the pleasure of gaining such elevated connections. When the silence continued the older man accepted that his son's unimpressive manner and modest fortune scarcely reflected his aristocratic birth, while Fitzwilliam Darcy's bearing and address were outstanding; he was not a man to be intimidated by higher rank. Caroline's suppressed excitement probably stemmed from disappointed hopes in that direction; no wonder she was enjoying the triumph of becoming a Duchess. But the story was so predictable that bringing this land deal to a satisfactory conclusion offered more satisfaction. He would offer half the initial payment - then he need do no more for James who was a good enough fellow, but a great bore.

After a short discussion it was agreed Darcy would pay the other half without any encroachment on the bride's capital. There was no objection to her private income helping to repay the mortgage.

James Scott's anxiety to continue his journey south restricted the joint celebrations to a few days. With having to organise his household as well as his estate it would be at least two months before he could get back to Pemberley to claim his bride, while his father, free of daily responsibilities, would marry within weeks. Both ceremonies would be equally quiet, the Duke making it clear he neither intended to be present at his son's marriage nor expected his son's presence at his own.

❧

Scene Twelve

❧

Scott returned to Derbyshire somewhat anxious about taking his bride from the luxurious spaces of Pemberley to a house of modest dimensions, and with a housekeeper used only to catering for a bachelor who rarely entertained. But natural confidence was rapidly restored; Littlefields was the home of a gentleman, and everything indoors as well as outdoors proclaimed it.

Georgiana was determined to be satisfied with all the existing arrangements, but it must be admitted that her lack of domestic experience weakened this optimistic assessment. Fortunately, as Scott's clearer grasp of reality had already determined that changes must be made, they were soon happily marking his sketch of the house with extensive additions such as nurseries above and a spacious drawing room below, thus transforming the existing parlour into her sitting-room. Months of upheaval were inevitable, but no walls of the existing house need be disturbed until the extension was complete. James suggested Georgiana might even enjoy supervising the work.

She knew she would! Her brother's long established habit of overseeing any alterations to her apartments at Pemberley, had become increasingly frustrating. For example, that octagonal sitting room off the upper lobby would have been a delightful project for her Pemberley summer (when time tended to pass slowly) but force of habit had led Darcy to act without further discussion. Redecoration had been completed before her arrival; the only flaw in the elegant new boudoir was that her own plans could not be implemented. How could she ever explain such feelings to her brother?

Reflecting on this, she was exhilarated by the thought that she and James would design all these additions to their home, but almost immediately, her usual diffidence reasserted itself and she began to feel that in this larger project some initial advice might be welcome. Perhaps the infinitely practical Mrs Fitzwilliam should be consulted? This naïve idea was a temporary lapse from her usual good understanding of James Scott's independent spirit. In fact the suggestion was so sharply dismissed as to revive an earlier suspicion that he disliked the lady. It was a thought too uncomfortable to contemplate further.

There was no need for the bride and groom to be heavily involved in wedding preparations. Pemberley retainers, who had been close to Georgiana all her life, would be at the church, but her other guests were limited to people closely bound by ties of friendship or kinship. Some of the strongest relationships had developed in the last two years: her admirable chaperon, Mrs Annesley, the Gervases, and a few musical friends – among whom she would have liked to include Dominic Cartwright had he still been in England. Georgiana, equally attached to mother and son, was particularly pleased that Mrs Cartwright's remarriage had settled her near Littlefields where they could meet without exposing Darcy to her company. Unused to finding fault with her brother, this recently developed distaste for such delightful people almost forced her to question his judgement.

Since her brother's marriage, the hitherto limited range of her affections had expanded to include those less alarming objects of love, Elizabeth and Cecilia.

Gaining so much from this new family (among whom she included the Bingleys) she longed to give James the happiness he had been denied by the repulsive indifference of his father and elder siblings. To her mind it was bad enough that the Duke chose to absent himself from the wedding, but even worse that only three people would represent that numerous family - his younger brothers and the elderly cousin, who had dutifully (if rather against his inclination) raised them. Scott chose to invite no one else, arguing that, as his few close acquaintances were all near Littlefields, a homecoming celebration would be more appropriate.

With Elizabeth's encouragement Georgiana had gained in self-assurance during the past year but her nature would never be generally gregarious. She had assumed social life was easier for men, and that James, with the advantage of being out in the world for several years, would have a greater number of friends. It seemed not to be the case; apparently many people were intimidated by his taciturn manners, while she had never felt nervous in his company. Mrs Annesley had noted, with surprise, the confident demeanour displayed by a girl usually so hesitant, but Georgiana herself was in no doubt of the reason. They were both immediately drawn to each other and their feelings intensified rapidly, although on the surface their courtship was tediously formal. Henry Fitzwilliam had quickly sensed this while Darcy continued to brood over Scott's possible deficiencies as an affectionate husband.

Mr Gervase was to perform the ceremony, bringing his wife and sisters as warmly invited guests. Georgiana's decision to have no attendant other than her dear sister, Elizabeth, relieved Darcy's fear that those pleasant young women, Maria and Bella Porter, might be unsuitably elevated to the position of bridesmaids. The fact that Maria, his own particular favourite, was to marry young Biggs, a tenant farmer, already threatened the social structures he had always regarded as immutable. Biggs was an admirable young man, much to be commended for bringing increased prosperity to Pleasant Valley Farm, but Darcy was not anxious to receive him at Pemberley – though the situation would be complicated when Maria Porter became his wife.

The Earl and Countess of Otterburn and their family were invited to Georgiana's wedding as a matter of course, but with little expectation that all of them would appear at the ceremony. As joint guardian, privy to all the arrangements, the Colonel (and his bride) would certainly be present, but the heir and his wife were abroad. Now the Earl's reply had been received and was unenthusiastically described by Darcy.

"I suppose we should be thankful the Otterburns will, after all, be at the wedding."

"You mean there will actually be a reconciliation?" asked Elizabeth, surprised that her husband looked grim and her sister uneasy. "If so, Georgiana, it will give you great pleasure to be the means of bringing it about."

"My aunt has written to me," she replied, "with most affectionate wishes for my happiness, but referring to our uncle's letter for details of their arrival."

"The letter comes from my uncle," said Darcy, "because an honourable woman like the Countess can only be heartily ashamed of the subterfuges in which they have involved themselves. Her old friend, Theodora Hunt, is in failing health, so they are already at Huntleigh with her, continuing to Pemberley late on the eve of the wedding and returning to Huntleigh immediately after the ceremony. It will require a degree of unseemly manoeuvring to avoid any contact with Mrs

Fitzwilliam, but possibly it will be achieved. This behaviour is more suited to one of the Earl's clandestine assignations, and he will receive minimal assistance from me."

Darcy, true to a belief that unmarried girls should not be sheltered from all knowledge of the world, had recently alluded, in general terms, to the licentious behaviour of their uncle and his heir, considering it better for Georgiana to hear first from him information that unctuous gossips would be sure to embroider for her benefit.

"It can hardly be considered a joyous reconciliation," conceded Georgiana. "But it is true, Elizabeth, that I am gratified my marriage will bring them all together for the first time. Such an encounter, however brief, must open the way to other meetings between a mother and son so dearly attached to each other."

Elizabeth agreed.

"Yes, when they meet face to face, I cannot believe the Countess will be able to rebuff him – though it is beyond my imagination to envisage any exchange of civilities between her and Mrs Fitzwilliam. The situation seems impossible of solution."

Darcy was in the discouraging position of not being much better pleased with his other aunt, Lady Catherine de Bourgh, though her recent, apparently uncharacteristic, action might in general terms be regarded as extending an olive branch. Unfortunately, her nephew judged the decision - to recognise Mrs Fitzwilliam - as the vulgar triumph of curiosity over animosity, despite Georgiana's plea that genuine family feeling might be involved.

Thinking it both convenient and intriguing to be entertained by the Fitzwilliams at Tollington Place while inspecting Georgiana's new home, Lady Catherine informed Henry Fitzwilliam of her readiness to be his guest, with no more than a cursory nod to the woman she thought of as 'that draper's assistant'. A more seemly recognition was forced from her. The Colonel, having spoken cheerfully but firmly of 'my wife's house', Mrs Fitzwilliam then required every detail of the proposed visit to be explained to herself as hostess.

"You are anxious to visit us at Tollington in the near future? My husband's guests, be they family or friends, are always welcome, just let me know what dates you have in mind."

Lady Catherine brusquely indicated that it would suit her to continue from Pemberley to Tollington.

"Ah, you envisage returning to with us in a few days time? The Housekeeper shall be notified immediately; have you any needs or preferences of which she should be forewarned? Please do not concern yourself about the lack of advance warning; unceremonious behaviour from a member of the family does not trouble me."

Colonel Fitzwilliam, mentally comparing the cheerful condescension shown to his unmannerly aunt with the aggressive replies to Elizabeth Darcy's well-intentioned greetings some months ago, admired the speed with which his wife was adjusting to her new society. Lady Catherine was silenced. She wished to be received at Tollington, and knew, from past experience with Darcy, that a nephew could ruthlessly break with an aunt over criticism of his wife. She had found the temporary loss of *that* connection extremely painful, and was in no mood to repeat the experience. Not a woman given to reflection, she failed to admit the loss had been self-imposed, nor did she examine the fact that her attitude to Darcy's wife had now changed from virulent dislike to something almost approaching approval.

With all these difficulties to be negotiated, it could not fail to be a great consolation to Lady Catherine that Georgiana's husband was highly acceptable. The evening before the wedding, Elizabeth heard her Ladyship interrogate her niece about Littlefields, beginning with an admonition that the plebeian name must certainly be changed. She received cautious answers from a bride newly alert to her bridegroom's dislike of outside 'meddling' and therefore reluctant to describe their own plans or respond to any suggestions. As Lady Catherine refused to understand that the existing house contained only one good sized parlour in addition to the dining-parlour and estate office, Georgiana received advice suited to the fictional establishment deemed appropriate for the alliance of an heiress with a son of the nation's wealthiest Duke. So far, reflected Elizabeth, her aunt had not dictated to Georgiana the exact arrangements of shelves and closets that Charlotte Collins had been forced to endure, but as her Ladyship would soon be calling at Littlefields the escape was likely to be only temporary.

The Otterburns' arrival having been announced for an unsociably late hour, everyone except their son and the Darcys had already retired. Equally careful timing ensured their arrival at the church a scant minute before the bride entered on the arm of her brother. Henry Fitzwilliam led his parents to their seats before taking his place between his wife and his mother. On this occasion for his own comfort he wished he were a bulkier man! However, the smallest gesture of a bow passed between the Otterburns and their daughter-in-law, thus avoiding a positive denial of Mrs Fitzwilliam.

When the ceremony ended, the rules of precedence enabled the Earl and Countess to be the first to follow the bride and groom as they left the church.

Immediately outside the porch they offered hasty congratulations, and (having said goodbye to other family members before the ceremony) turned to enter their carriage. They were not fast enough; the Darcys and Lady Catherine emerged from the church and they must all bear the discomfort of a few more minutes in each other's company. Henrietta Otterburn looked so ill that Elizabeth impulsively stepped forward to correct the cold manner of their earlier farewells. The older woman, larger in height and girth, warmly embraced her, saying emphatically.

"You are a good girl and richly deserve your happy marriage. May Georgiana be as fortunate."

Within moments the Otterburns' carriage had left. Pride of birth had motivated the shabby behaviour that made Fitzwilliam Darcy hope his 'noble' aunt and uncle at least experienced some of the shame he felt on their behalf. Elizabeth could well imagine the pain felt by the Countess as she watched the gratifying union of her niece with the son of a Duke, while sitting in alienating silence beside her own son and his unacceptable wife. Alas, however intense Lady Otterburn's sufferings no meaningful gesture of reconciliation had been offered.

Following the wedding breakfast the general farewells were made, then, at the door of the carriage, Georgiana embraced her brother and his wife before setting off with her husband for a life, which she hoped, might almost equal theirs in happiness.

From the moment they were engaged, Elizabeth had urged Darcy to overlook Lady Catherine's intemperate and arrogant intrusion into their lives. This civilised action had not affected her disdain for Darcy's aunt, whose invitation to the wedding was solely a matter of duty. It happened however, that, following her arrival and without any apparent justification, Elizabeth began to feel more tolerant. Indeed this new sensation was uncomfortably close to pity – and what could be more provoking than having to relinquish a well-justified dislike?

It was not that Lady Catherine's manners were noticeably improved, but when she embarked on her usual unfavourable assessment of Elizabeth's attainments compared with those of her daughter, Anne, a sudden vision of the sickly creature whose weak health would probably deteriorate over the years, awoke a pang of sympathy for the mother's unreasonable claims. They were discourteous and unnecessary but almost certainly dictated as much by defensive maternal love as family pride. What lonely months they must spend together at Rosings, with no greater distraction available to this energetic woman than prying into the lives of all the de Bourgh dependents.

No wonder Elizabeth's feelings softened as she watched her husband help a vigorously wriggling Cecilia balance for a moment on his knees, while his aunt warned that the child would certainly develop bandy legs. When Darcy's only response was to smile and shake his head, she raised her voice even more to announce that Mrs Collins had been wise enough to benefit from the warning. The sound of her own voice mistakenly convinced Lady Catherine of an attentive audience but, as it happened, Cecilia's delight in this new game absorbed all her father's attention, providing a welcome distraction from the melancholy afflicting him since Georgiana's departure.

Darcy considered it unmanly to display such feelings to anybody, least of all to Elizabeth, but the effort to dissemble created a chilling air of reserve. This was regarded as normal behaviour by guests with whom he was little acquainted, accepted philosophically by his cousin, who was suffering his own miseries, ignored by his aunt, and silently endured by his wife whose instinctive wish to offer comfort was inhibited by a reluctance to imply that her presence was consolation enough for the loss of the young sister so long entrusted to his care.

They misunderstood each other – Darcy's low spirits were not caused by his own loss, but by the fear that Georgiana's marriage would be denied the blessings that had transformed his own life. As is often the case in a happy union, such a misunderstanding did not long survive the privacy of their own rooms where, after one uncommunicative night, Elizabeth found a sense of delicacy was no match for her need to be a comforting wife. After a few sentences acknowledging the sense of loss he must be suffering, she continued,

"But I want to show the same tenderness to you that you always give to me, please let me..."

Incredulity made Darcy take hold of his wife.

"I discourage the tenderness which creates my greatest happiness? How can you think this?"

Elizabeth returned his kiss before further explanation.

"I expressed myself badly: let me substitute another word, 'solicitude'. You respond so lovingly when you feel I lack spirits or am overtired." (She chose to banish the recollection of occasions when these attentions seemed excessive) "Let me help you in the same way. You cannot think my wish to give comfort is less than yours."

There was no arguing with such a plea. When Elizabeth learned that his low spirits were caused by the belief that James Scott was unworthy of Georgiana, she offered such thoughtfully reasoned arguments as almost to persuade Darcy that Scott, already bearing an exemplary character in society, was likely to prove a devotedly attentive husband, with all his affections centred on his domestic life. She finished by making a comparison between tensions caused by her relatives, and Darcy's current distaste for James Scott.

"For my sake you have shown great forbearance towards certain members of my family. On Georgiana's behalf I know you would willingly do as much, but in the belief that Scott will also make a great effort, I hope that more will not be required of you. This cheerful prophecy does not include the expectation that you two will ever much like each other, but at least a civil compromise will be reached."

As Darcy did not dispute any of these points she made another request causing equal surprise.

"In other areas - quite unconnected with Georgiana - I sometimes fear you are greatly troubled, although you never admit it. In short, while I fail to disguise from you anxiety or exhaustion, I suspect you keep either or both of these conditions from me."

"But I am always well," he responded in genuine surprise. "And while I am delighted that in general this also applies to you, I claim one small (or perhaps I should say large) advantage; physically I am stronger, therefore unlikely to become seriously fatigued as sometimes happens when you overestimate your powers of endurance. Other than that incontrovertible fact I claim just two more advantages over you: a superior command of worldly knowledge, and the husband's accepted role as protector of his wife and children." With a touch of irony, he enquired, " Have you a particular weakness in mind for me?"

"Heaven forbid! It is just a general observation that although you involve me in much of the overall management of Pemberley, there are other occasions when you emerge from the estate office noticeably worried. You appear weary and distracted for hours afterwards; are there burdens that I fail to comprehend through lack of business acumen?"

"Nonsense my dear. While agreeing that complicated accounts are not your strength, the fact is of no importance; I keep an accountant for that. Believe me we are as prosperous and flourishing as anyone can be in these unsettled times, nevertheless your perceptions almost hit the mark. I am concerned about the unprecedented speed of the changes taking place in our society. We have both realised that the end of the French Wars will bring bad as well as good results, most notably when discharged soldiers swell the number of workmen already competing with the new machines. In industrial areas the existing hostility towards employers can only increase. Pemberley, although unlikely to be centrally involved, cannot remain entirely unaffected, and I foresee a future when the people who work for me become almost equally distrustful.

"Yet I must hope, I do hope, that in the long term these inventions – the product of remarkable minds – will be for the benefit of mankind. The problem for our family is that the old ways were good ways for landowners, yet change they must, and I see no way to influence events. My black moods illustrate a somewhat ignoble characteristic – I crave action but am powerless to act, creating a sense of frustration hard for me to bear. Undoubtedly I must learn to control those feelings, and you must waste no further sympathy on me."

After pondering these words, Elizabeth urged various good reasons for Darcy discussing his feelings with her, concluding with, "I shall gain insight from your greater knowledge, and you will have the dubious benefit of my opinions, for you may be certain I shall produce my own vision of a future which cannot yet be foreseen with complete accuracy. The need to dissuade me from some of my views will be more constructive than solitary brooding."

Her last words persuaded her husband to smile, and admit that perhaps she was right, though both were aware that his urge to control events was unlikely to change.

The remaining guests departed the following day, leaving only Lady Catherine and the Fitzwilliams to benefit from their host's improved demeanour, which was softened even further by receiving (earlier than he expected) a letter from Georgiana written en-route for Dorset. After factual details of the journey she expressed, at greater length, her gratitude to her brother for years of loving care, and to both of them for demonstrating so clearly the beauty of domestic happiness. She and James, united by mutual love and shared interests, hoped to deserve the same felicity. Darcy, deeply moved, once more felt he might be able to accept his sister's choice of James Scott, and even managed to tolerate the heartfelt praise for her husband with which Georgiana concluded her letter.

The Bingleys had missed the wedding due to Jane suffering a few days nausea – so far unexplained, though Lady Catherine did not hesitate to voice everyone's guess that it might herald another pregnancy. But now those dearest of all friends had arrived for a visit that would continue after the Fitzwilliams carried this troublesome aunt off to Tollington in a few days time.

Her departure would free the Darcys and the Bingleys to discuss their own future visits to Dorset, that distant county which was to be home to Georgiana as well as Charles' natural daughter, Penelope. While the Bingleys still assumed they would all share summer lodgings, Darcy had developed more ambitious ideas; he planned to purchase a place in Dorset, if possible, resembling Lyme Lodge, but situated about ten miles beyond Lyme Regis. Positive action connected with Georgiana's life would be a pleasure, but for the present he could do no more than initiate enquiries. In all likelihood Henry Fitzwilliam would hospitably invite everyone to Tollington, but the Bingleys (unrelated to the Fitzwilliams) would demur, and for the Darcys, a long stay with Mrs Fitzwilliam might be uncongenial, not to mention the greater disadvantage of General and Mrs Tollington as immediate neighbours.

Darcy had an additional interest in purchasing an estate in Dorsetshire. It was to be a present for Elizabeth; a secret he meant to keep until the ideal place had been found. Everyone Darcy loved was to benefit by this project, not only his wife and sister, but in the distant future, Cecilia - Darcy being convinced Elizabeth would wish her property to go to her eldest daughter. Naturally his masculine confidence felt no doubt they would raise a family somewhere between four and six in number and comprising both sexes. He felt certain Pemberley would not lack a male heir. Indeed his main concern remained, as always, the fear that too many children would weaken his wife's health.

While genuinely grateful that a well-beloved guardian would be Georgiana's near neighbour, it pained him to know that over the years he must cede to Henry Fitzwilliam the task of watching over his sister's welfare if her husband proved negligent in any way. It would be a great advantage to own a place in the southwest, though he would like to avoid leaving Pemberley during its most beautiful seasons.

Darcy was not yet fully persuaded that James Scott could be other than selfish, but unknown to him, even now the young husband was preparing to make a generous gesture on behalf of his wife. He had determined to accept that Higgins woman, improperly raised from draper's assistant to the status of Mrs Fitzwilliam. In any other circumstances he would have refused to receive her at Littlefields, but was setting aside his own wishes not only for Georgiana's sake, but also for Colonel Fitzwilliam, a man infinitely more agreeable than Fitzwilliam Darcy. From the start he would make it clear this concession did not extend to any interference in his married life from the vulgar Mrs Fitzwilliam. This embargo was also to be extended to that aristocratic busybody, Lady Catherine.

The days following Georgiana's departure were brightened for her brother by the presence of the Bingleys – who helpfully inspired a new scheme with which the Darcys could be immediately busy. Working on a shared project was a source of happiness to them both.

Charles, in his usual self-deprecatory manner, described his progress in estate management.

"Riding across the fields with Jefferson and his brother is good fun but, idle fellow that I am, I don't attend closely enough to details, making me deservedly the dunce of the class when we get back to the Estate Office. Young Jefferson, although a Naval man, sees everything I have missed and offers useful suggestions far beyond my capacity."

"You forget my dear," said his loyal wife, "that all this is new to you, while Captain Jefferson grew up at Wychwood, and what is more it has remained his home whenever he is ashore. But will he really be able to manage a place of his own with one leg amputated at the knee? The cheerful face he presents to the world is almost beyond praise."

"Yes, he is a remarkable man, commanding not only respect but the warmest affection. His brother and sister are determined that when he moves it must be to a place reasonably near them, but even so are reluctant to lose him. However, despite his youthfully ingenuous air, I know he wishes to be settled as soon as maybe, and is amazingly confident of managing independently. When the three of us are out together he either rides an old horse at a walking pace or drives a sturdy gig, but it is alarming to contemplate even a minor upset. It would never be safe for him to go out on his own."

"He will greatly depend on the right choice of steward," suggested Darcy, who already had an idea he wished to share with his wife about this young man's future. For the moment he spoke to the assembled group only about young Jefferson's need for an assistant combining youthful strength with a degree of experience - and if possible the personal qualities to provide agreeable companionship.

It was comfortably agreed among them all that the steward (particularly on a small estate) not infrequently became a friend of the family. It could also happen on large estates without necessarily proving a blessing, thought Darcy, remembering his father's affection for the Wickhams, father and son, and regretting his own introduction of the word 'companionship'.

As soon as he was alone with Elizabeth, he propounded at some length a plan to offer Jefferson the property previously held in reserve for their cousin, Colonel Fitzwilliam.

Elizabeth was delighted.

Where could we find anyone more deserving of help, and more likely to become our valued friend? Only an exceptional spirit could appear so amiable and unpretending while enduring all the restrictions that amputation imposes on a vigorous young man. Everything seems to be in favour of your excellent idea, my dear, generous, husband, unless something about Grove End makes it utterly unsuitable – steep hills and valleys suited only to a mountain pony, or a house with a narrow corkscrew staircase and not enough rooms to provide a master bedroom downstairs."

Her husband awaited further explanation of these wild suppositions.

"These unlikely fantasies are just to underline the fact you have not yet taken me to see the place, which I imagine to somewhat resemble Longbourn as to the size of the house and the amount of farming land. I have a great curiosity about it; how soon can we go?"

Darcy, preferring it to be a surprise, replied to the final question without offering any further details.

"Wait just a few days until the Fitzwilliams and Lady Catherine have left. There are obvious reasons for excluding the latter, and with my cousin I would be uncomfortable about the fact he was inspecting a property originally destined for him."

"But he knows nothing at all of this."

"And that circumstance would involve me in a degree of artifice. It is altogether more suitable we go there only with the Bingleys."

His wife replied,"I entirely agree, not least because it offers the significant advantage of avoiding Lady Catherine's comments! There was a time when I judged Mrs Fitzwilliam to be equally domineering, but the confidence provided by a happy marriage has made her wonderfully less acerbic. Nowadays it is amazing how moderate I consider your cousin's wife when measured against your aunt."

"And this," replied Darcy, "despite the persuasive arguments you offer as an excuse for my aunt's hectoring manners? Although you have made me feel more sympathetic, I still regret the number of visits likely to be inflicted upon us in future, in addition to the even less agreeable prospect of the annual visit to Rosings."

"Do you so much dislike a visit there?" enquired Elizabeth who felt it would provide the easiest circumstances for enjoying the company of Charlotte while enduring that of Mr Collins.

Her husband chose not to pursue the point. Mrs Bennet, at an unwary moment during her recent visit, had disclosed Mr Collins' condescending intention of marrying Elizabeth, emphasising that he naturally had no doubt of the offer being gratefully accepted. The anecdote was meant to show that Lizzie had not lacked suitors, but tailed into incoherence when her son-in-law's glacial look awoke fears that Lizzy might already have told him everything – including her own maternal insistence the proposal be accepted. Not unusually, Mrs Bennet was mistaken; it was not a subject Elizabeth would ever raise with Darcy, and he was equally silent about his newly acquired knowledge. Inwardly he continued to be revolted that such a man had not only dared to entertain the idea, but had been confident of success while he himself had to amend his faults before earning her regard. The situation might have been eased if both man and wife had shown less delicacy; Mr Collins as an oafish figure of fun would be easier for Darcy to endure than his present feelings of disgust. Noting her husband's frown and compressed lips Elizabeth did not trouble to repeat her original question about Rosings, but accepted an oblique reply.

"It is greatly to your credit that you have managed to overcome the unjustified hostility of both these women, but as far as our own pleasure is concerned the prime advantage is comfortable contact with the Fitzwilliams."

Within a space of hours Elizabeth saw Darcy's sympathy fully tested. Lady Catherine, having captured him in a corner from which escape was impossible, was voicing her disapproval of various changes made at Pemberley since his marriage. Unaware of his wife's sympathetic glance, his countenance had changed from the cheerfulness of domestic ease to the gloomily dutiful air of a nephew listening to an overbearing aunt.

"Now Darcy, as your mother's only sister I stand almost in a parental role and have a right to be attended to, particularly now I am reconciled to your marriage. Your wife's family we will *not* discuss but considering the antecedents of Mrs Fitzwilliam (not to mention her social ineptitude) Mrs Darcy is increasingly acceptable. The outspoken opinions she has always voiced so readily are fortunately more appropriate to the wife of Fitzwilliam Darcy than they were to a chit of a girl with neither fortune nor family to recommend her."

Such faint praise displeased Darcy, who was about to remonstrate, had not his aunt's next words gone some way towards redeeming her earlier ones.

"Although I admit to somewhat enjoying your wife's company, that does not mean I approve the changes being initiated at Pemberley. Presumably you are still master here, so why allow a noticeable slackening of the standards always upheld by my sister, Lady Anne? To my mind it suggests a lack of the filial respect due to your mother's memory. For example, I suspect a sharp reduction in the number of footmen on duty, and the one outside my apartments I certainly caught leaning against the wall – if not nodding off. Nor is that the only…"

Fortunately, for the moment it was the only complaint she had time to voice, for all the house guests were assembling for a drive round the park, supposedly under the direction of Henry Fitzwilliam, but Lady Catherine was in no doubt her recollections and recommendations would be needed.

This left the Darcys free to stroll down the grassy slope to the ornamental bridge, now in need of repair. On this spot, more than a year ago, Elizabeth first realised that Mrs Cartwright had been her husband's mistress during the months after he and Bingley left Netherfield to escape the dangerous charms of the two eldest Miss Bennets. How bitterly and irrationally jealous she had been and how painful the estrangement. Now their only concern was to plan the reconstruction of the bridge. Darcy inclined to a straightforward rebuilding in its present rustic style while Elizabeth felt it was perfectly situated to make chinoiserie a delightful change.

This inconclusive debate soon gave way to talking of their great good fortune. Not only was their marriage blessed by a healthy baby, but an additional source of happiness was having the Bingleys – and their pleasant neighbours – within reasonable reach. With a variety of plans and projects to work at together, and assuming everyone continued in good health, they could foresee no greater troubles in their married life than encounters with their more tiresome relatives, or a disagreement about their relationship with Maria Porter in her new role as Mrs Biggs.

The wider world presented greater problems, but as there can be no savour in a life without difficulties, they were likely to fulfil the joyful boast made by Elizabeth when they were first engaged:

"It is settled between us already that we are to be the happiest married couple in the world."

The End

235

The Darcys – Scenes from Married Life

Email:books@egertonhousepublishing.co.uk